I0618737

Tempting Fiction

Les Cook

Published by Les Cook, 2022.

Fiction

Intended for a Mature Audience

Over 18 Years of age.

Copyright © Les Cook

Published 2022

Contact: Les Cook

Lescook360@gmail.com

Library and Archives Canada:

395 Wellington Street. Ottawa ON. KIA 0N4

Paperback ISBN 978-1-9990023-4-3

Digital ISBN 978-1-9990023-2-9

Table of Contents

Context

Prologue

—————

A selection of tales.

Connected or disconnected, as you like.

Library Girl

EATING CANTALOUPES in the middle of autumn like its summertime. I can't afford them, but I'll eat them. Tchaikovsky 6th symphony today and I don't feel better or worse. Lazy – is that the bread of winter?

I can't spare change and I avoid the sight of work. Three lines at a time and then wait for more words . . . proof of existence – therapy?

The Beatles are boring and poets weak. Am I to die a lonely man?

Nobody stops or steps my way. Ridiculous is the poet. Fragment or fragmented sentences are my pleasure. Rage against what – some monk on the hills of Tibet? I cry I'll never die and never will I force food down another's throat. Soups hot on the stove; safe to say I'll find my library card after dining alone today.

I have no idea where this is going – it's like a piece of art. 1990 is next – I'm not twenty-four years old yet.

I make the bed and find a costume for this night. The outfit will be a black toque, black leather gloves, and a kimono with dead fish pressed on. I lie on my bed thinking of my most recent poem and pencil in slight changes. It's a poem of how one should be quiet when chorusing another . . . the use of a flute on a snake, you may say.

She's here, the knock on my door is light . . . the girl I met at the library, a bookworm with plentiful hips and a sexy ass. I can't say I'm proud of her, only proud that she comes here near midnight on any given night. In ten years she'll fall apart, her amazing protruding butt and breasts will no longer be flattery. She's smart though, getting her licks in now. She is frightened as I bend over her with my toque covering my face, gloves, and kimono on; it's the truth though . . . I might as well pretend I'm raping her physically because I certainly am mentally.

We're on break and she wants to smoke; I allow her to. In time I'm fucking her backwards with my hands holding her feet. My eyes look forward towards the knife near the edge of my mattress.

It isn't any use; I'm not to come in her again. Just before my dry orgasm I pick up the knife at the end of the mattress and slit her big toe open. At first, she doesn't seem to feel the blood leak . . . a delayed reaction. She doesn't even scream. I eject confused.

She pulls the toe trickling blood up to her face. With a small unrehearsed smirk she says, "What have you done?"

'A favour, I've done you a favour,' I answer rolling to the edge of the bed in hope of delayed redemption.

'I'm bleeding, did you do that on purpose?' she asks.

'I just got carried away.'

All seems calm; she's still examining her toe with some type of weird diplomacy.

'Do you think I should go to emergency?' A concealed euphoria is in her.

'You're okay,' I answer. 'I'll find you a bandage.' This little wound should have rid her of me but she sits unsettled treating the cut as a tattoo.

'No more knives, do you agree? I can't believe you cut my toe.'

She says this as a fair treaty.

I walk away for a bandage and find myself in the shower. 'Oh girl with the cut toe, please go. I want to fall in love,' is what I sing in the shower. She's still in bed with only her sore toe free of the covers. She's monitoring the toe like a baby sheep. I can't contain my humour. 'Did you like that?'

'Yeah, I did, in a bizarre sort of way. It's not something I'd like done again, but I like my little scar on my toe. I won't forget you now.' She's exhilarated . . . I fear she wants more sex.

'You must leave. I have to be at work early tomorrow morning,' I concede.

Her expression says everything. She dresses and calls me a prick, claiming that I'd probably cut her toe on purpose to get rid of her.

If that isn't enough, she wants to know my plans for the weekend.

I refuse to answer.

'Enough now, get going, I need to sleep,' is my only speech. She leaves. I stay awake and write. My benefactor wants results. My benefactor is Claire Martin. It's Claire Martin's townhouse where I live and her money that I live on.

I haven't a mind to write conversation or dialect. Don't think everything is pretty and quaint; I live in some lazy town. . . although the mountain scenery and small lakes are nice. An upscale to everything!

Raking the fall leaves at Claire's like an imbecile, and what's the pay? Whatever she decides, maybe dinner with her, a bottle of wine, twenty bucks, or just maybe a big fat "you're living in my rental for free", or all of the above on a good day. I can however swing this in my disturbed mind as exercise . . . yes, fresh air. The swishing of leaves as they've done for thousands of years. A half hour has gone by and the wind has begun to leave the air in a frozen state. The leaves – they'll be here tomorrow another hour is all I can stand. I'll push for two hours and the front yard shall be done. So much for gas in the car, four hours of work will surely call for a little of her cash, but two hours of work is all but a favour.

Here comes Claire just as I'm to quit. She's with a man.

Claire freed me from living with the dregs of society where I'd wash walls for free beer on Sundays and cook cocaine for amateurs so I'd have food and drink during the week. I'd sleep on the floor in a large closet off the hall; method writing, a dreadful idea.

I met Claire on a good day at the Passport office (I wasn't going anywhere, but she didn't know that) I had on nice shoes; the shoes and the passport office sold me. Instant trust, we shared a drunken night – she thought I was someone. I wrote her a poem. I hinted, 'I need help . . . I live the life of a saint in hell, please let me out. I only want to cut and paste words; write, chop, and not explain.'

She agreed. I raced away and retrieved dollars I'd stashed for an escape. I bought a car. Claire had done well as a homeowner. She'd profited in the buy, sell, and rental game. She gave me an option, full-time writing and a place to stay in exchange for keeping an eye on her rental complex and the odd job here and there for a little cash. I'd have to cater to her a bit, one of the fine quirks. Our future outlook is of a duo publishing my work and others. Claire delights in the imaginative thought of moulding and erecting an artist, her closing immortalized in story. She can live forever on the pages of a book.

A rather nice home I stay in, has two bedrooms, two floors. My official position is Claire's assistant. Claire is a writer herself, but she never makes time for her dream, she'd rather live it out through me. We've swapped a lot of poems late in the night.

Claire isn't to woo me today, she has a date, they're jolly, hugging, and kissing. 'Don't introduce me' is what I think. I don't want to meet the man she'll cheat. She only waves, and he says 'Hello.' I decide to finish raking the backyard.

I should have been a poet: what a life that would be, if I was rich I'd write poems and if I was poor I'd write poems, and in-between I'd experience! What else is there in life but poems, nothing else makes sense. And when I die, my bones will be left and my skin pecked away in a desert where I'll decay in a ditch with a leg on the road. Dead, no funeral, no celebration. Grief is a moment as a stranger pass by, leave me alone, let me disintegrate in the ground and fly to the sky; yes, and leave this rather nice rake, it will be my mark or sight, please no stone, just this rake as my place of death.

When I'm done the raking, I don't knock at Claire's door. I walk away and find my car to burn the last of my fuel away. Fuel to view a little city, personalities of cheap paint, comical but once in a while you find a special girl demanding and planning an escape, and that's what I'm looking for. I've been keeping a bottle of wine for her. I drive around downtown. The imaginary girl isn't out today, which leaves me to debate. Should I write about green grass even though it's yellow, shall I describe in great detail the style of the man's shirt or the sediment of downtown? Well, I can do all this in one word, the word is 'stale'.

Claire phones, she's sporting a good mood. 'What's up,' she speaks.

'Broke.' I needn't say more, Claire has my next paycheck figured out.

'I can't talk about it over the phone, and you can't come over because I have friends here.'

'That guy, is he still there?'

'Oh no, I got rid of him but I have some friends over. I'll see you tomorrow; I'll pick you up for lunch. No, I'll bring lunch, what do you want?'

'Something filling, surprise me.'

Noon has past, Claire's awfully late and hunger has set; it's the torture of waiting for someone that starves a person. Damage to my nerves . . . what is the pay for that? A day has drizzled away, I write little unable to indulge wholly.

Claire hands me seafood pasta. She speaks with sporadic foresight and prompt insight. I eat as her hand clasps my knee. Hawaii, that's her fluster . . . abbreviated thoughts and emotions, she's flying . . . Maui, a three-week vacation, and she's leaving in a week. Her and the man she was so happily performing with yesterday. I still haven't caught his name or perspective for that matter, other than they're friends.

When my takeout is over and her breath has ceased, the only thing that concerns me is eight hundred dollars. Eight hundred – the number of dollars I get for doing near nothing. Answer her phone, take notes and complaints, drop a few errands, and be her telephone cord to events. The use of her house: 'You'll get to watch television on the big screen and a fridge full of food.'

As her assistant, the pay isn't much and neither is the work. Claire's spreading the welfare around, how glorious, although I will have to spend a few afternoons with her this week, gathering information and duties, how marvellous. She'll leave me a couple hundred dollars before she leaves.

Democracy, if you vote for yourself enough... you'll have won. If you waiver and let others rule, you'll scowl. The servant is only happy when the servant is the happy servant, a position the servant has long cherished.

Two days have passed as I wait for Claire. I want to serve. Angry with the wait for Claire who provides me with free time and then takes it away. The burden of freedom is relying on another. Am I the smart artist or the desperate fool not aware he's playing on someone else's field?

Library Girl came by this afternoon, she wanted to stay, undress, and copulate, but I said, 'Let us go for a walk.' We drank tea at the mall, conversed and went our separate ways like our first encounter in the library at the end of summer.

Library Girl smiled that first time in the library, I responded uninhibited with delight. I spoke the words to let her pass, and she commented on all the books I held. I passed her on the road as she walked home – and this would be my path from the end of summer on.

Library Girl believes in occurrences, several times I'd passed by her in my car or by foot. She scheduled my route, found my house. She plotted for an interception on my daily route. I'd walk through the woods in the day for only the reason to see her. It isn't the woods so much as to where and when I leave the woods to the street near her home. On a day I'd forgotten about her (good thing, otherwise I might have had words too rehearsed) startled to find her a few feet from my eyes walking my way. Library Girl stopped in shock ecstasy, her eyes wide, her movement slightly backwards blowing. I grinned handsomely as I could. Will it finally happen – what we both thought in the library?

Honestly... she said, 'Are you just going for a walk or do you have somewhere in mind?'

I gave her a smile that matched. Library Girl didn't have anywhere in mind.

'Just walk, walk together,' I said.

Her smile continued and responded to the question.

We walked in silence. We walked straight to my house, walked in, put on tea.

She stood in front of the window commenting on the rain while backing to me. We embraced to the living room floor. Self-respect she must perceive, she struggled away. We were both still fully dressed, face against face, not even a kiss.

'You better let me go.' She joked.

'Go!'

'Okay.' And this is when we started kissing as we stood up.

'Go!' I commanded softly.

'I can't stop now. I want to stay.'

'Go and come back tomorrow morning at ten, we'll look at the words I write on paper. Go, go now, or I'll never let you go.'

'Tempting,' she said passionately.

She held me through slipping on shoes and turning the knob.

She did come in the morning but we only walked to the library and called it a day until the night.

Her desire deepened. She said she's always told the man what to do, now it's the man's turn. She eased into her outfit – clean, washed well, parked her car, not in my drive but nearby. Night, the soft romantic music swelled . . . no lights . . . we fucked all night, in the morning we conversed, made a date – we never do it the same.

Claire rang my bell, 'Let's go!' Of course, now that anticipation has killed my eagerness she shows up while I'm relaxing in my bed.

The details have been discussed: I'm to stay at her place the last night before she's to leave for her trip to Hawaii, her idea.

I don't bring much: a toothbrush, razor and cream, myself is what I bring. Claire is somewhat distressed, she walks hunched over and speaks little, the joking gone. As we look over some notes on her desk she lays her head against my chest. Her neck curves and her breasts lift, my lips soft and my hands kind. We bend over her desk methodical and speak nothing . . . the world has changed . . . just her and I. We rotate, we hold so tight, I come. We eat and spend the remainder of the night in bed, television. No sex she says, she's too sore.

Claire has an array of multicoloured bruises from the bottom of her butt to the top. The bruises are on her left side, sharp red stabs among blue, black, yellow colours. I can't ignore them any longer.

'How'd you get the huge bruises?'

She sits up and laughs, 'I fell down the steps really hard.'

'I'll bet . . . drunk?'

'Pissed,' she admits.

Claire is gone to Hawaii. I'm under no illusion of my plans with Claire. I'm with her to work. I wander around the kitchen and the living room, turning on the television and working at the computer, small tasks and I'm back in her bath.

In the next few days, I develop a habit of chatting to Library Girl on the phone. After an early evening telephone conversation with Claire, I decide it's time to see Library Girl.

Smelling so fresh, the bed made tight, set tranquil, before a storm of odour. I've made arrangements to have Library girl come to my place, not Claire's. Nothing equals a large sparse bedroom and that's what I have, no dresser, nothing . . . anything of value is in the closet. A sanctuary of echoes, a room that sounds silence bright with no abstractions as the room waits on motion, art, and science.

Decorations: we've all overdone them, only strict necessities are necessary.

Library Girl in a tone most polite, the door is open and she creeps up the stairs, dropping her jacket, unbuttoning her shirt;

all that we'd conspired earlier on the telephone. I stand behind the door as she walks in loosening away her shirt from her skirt. She grasps her bra in a stretch, the skirt unveiled, her legs walk her to the wall, she arches using her arms to support her back, and I observe her crotch. I walk naked and don't dare tear her panties down.

I drop to my knees and compliment the most courageous ass. I plunge splashing against her gash, my face affixed to stick.

Facing now, we back up onto the bed. She's soft like a willow, I'm overcome in rage to choke and punch her. I pull her hair to the side as she sighs, 'More!' I pull fierce as anger heats . . . I rip at the sheets, vicious energy gathers! 'Slap me, hit me,' I pant.

She's incoherent she won't do what she's told. I clench a fist and come with a slight punch to her face.

We don't stop! I exhaust myself. I'm confused, I've just punched her, not terrifically hard, but this won't be dismissed.

I slide to my side disturbed, satisfied. Immediately she flips on top, a red blemish around her eye. She's rampaging on me and I deflate, still in a zoo of personal contradiction, 'she'll hate me', I hate me.

'You can't fuck me now! You punched me, didn't you?' She's begun to cry, 'Fuck you!' she slaps me and folds over. She's gone to the mirror. I dress.

'Is this a common thing for you, to punch a woman?'

'I've never done that before. Listen. Come here please, so I can talk to you.'

'You're lucky it's not too bad.' She says nonchalant, her body is relaxed, she's fixing her hair. I sense we can get through this.

She sits beside me on the bed.

'Listen. This has been a progression.'

She smiles, 'Yes I know, you might not have meant to do it but you did.'

'Remember I choked you so hard you gasped and started fighting my arms. Again, I apologized and said I got carried away, but I knew what I was doing. I choked you until you couldn't stand it. Last time I slit your big toe open.'

'Yep,' she pulls her toe up to my face.

'You see what's happening, we can't see each other. I hold some kind of weird anger and passion towards you. I've never done any of these things to anyone before. Maybe I can't admit that I like you or refuse to admit it.'

'Well, you haven't hurt me yet, I don't know, but you scare me. I like that though. You make me crazy, even tonight I think "cool, maybe I'll have a little black eye from rough sex". That's sick, I'm sick because I'm still sitting here with you.' She's hoping to admire a slight black eye, I hope not.

Claire is back from Hawaii. After what she considers a hectic take charge day, she has time to visit with me. It isn't a visit it's the velvet rub off. She kisses my lips once, twice, only to stop herself and tell me she's in a relationship. She and her beau have decided that it is best if I move on. No more room, or work, or talk of books, I have to be out in two weeks. She'll shell out three hundred and fifty dollars for the inconvenience. For days I can see she's fought this, it isn't her decision, it's his. She says it's been a whirlwind affair, they haven't a plan to marry as yet.

'You can't find friends that easily,' I claim hostile. She only shrugs. I question, 'Is he that great?'

Claire's blocked me out, explaining she'll write out a check and leave it on her desk. I can leave my key behind when I pick up the check. There is no decision to be made on my part, I'm to leave tomorrow.

I miss Library Girl. I'll meet her before I leave.

I drive by Claire's place; her car is in the drive. I knock on the door and ring the bell.

No answer. I enter her key and take a chance . . . she did say she'd leave the check on her desk. I open the door and shout, 'Hello.'

I get a return, 'Hello,' from Claire. 'Come to my room,' she yells.

'Jesus Christ,' swearing like I'd seen him myself. Claire's tied up in ropes restrained to the bed. A rope wraps around her neck returning to her arms – ropes everywhere, I can't figure it out. Her ankles are tied to the front of the bed loose enough for her legs to bend.

She has a silk black nightgown on, her naked front exposed, no smile.

'Come fuck me,' she says.

'Claire, how long have you been like this?'

'Since this morning, now come fuck me . . . he wouldn't.'

'What, he just ties you up and leaves you here?'

She doesn't speak.

I don't want to laugh, it isn't funny.

'Don't talk, just come here.'

'I don't know if I can Claire.'

'Yeah you can, just come put it in my mouth for a while.' She speaks as if she's on her last breath. 'Come on just stick it here and touch me.'

'I shouldn't be doing this.' I'm hesitant and blow out a deep breath.

'Yeah you can, rub me,' she tells.

I tend to her, handing myself to her, in time I know I can fuck her.

As we start up, she tries raising her arms only to choke herself.

He's tied her arms so if she brings them up forward together, she chokes herself.

'Claire, keep your arms down,' I plead.

I struggle to hem her arms down as she scratches my wrist. I release her arms. She chokes herself by locking her arms around my neck.

In time I feel she hasn't the strength to release her arms. I break her lock. As we fuck harder, faster I lose control of her arms, she's choking. I can't continue. She's turning colours, gasping on the verge of strangulation. I rip away and plunge her arms down; she's completely out of breath. I attempt to untie her, she appeals, 'No.'

I retreat to the kitchen and discover a knife, and cut the rope to her arms and neck.

'Okay you win, now come fuck me,' her voice near gone.

'No Claire, I just want to pick up my check.'

'It's on my desk, go get it and then come fuck me.'

She's masturbating now, her legs still tied.

'Sorry, Claire.'

'At least tie me up for when he comes back,' her last words.

I walk out.

I thought I'd gotten rid of all the weirdo's this time, but I only attract them . . . time to find my humble beginnings.

We can switch so quick; I'd thought the ultimate of Claire, and now nothing. Once inside her my sights grew sane. She's a monstrous slave to her own pussy. It isn't me any unsuspecting man would do.

I may admit it was a sexy thing her being tied up, only I wasn't the one who'd done the tying. She's just too damn wretched to enjoy.

I told Library Girl the story, she listened, she didn't seem upset, fascinated really, her eyes bulged many times, maybe I have Library girl pegged wrong. I kissed her passionately today, frustration and kink gone. Library Girl, she's all right there's no real difference between me and her and Claire and me, unable to escape with the perfect mate we escape secretly with the help of each other. Limited fulfillment is preferred over none.

I cross the mountain pass, now on the prairies I place my writing book on my lap, and scribble as I drive. The long straight prairie roads are the best creation for a writer taking notes. No writing unless it's something fun. Screw a complicated text.

Glad I spent money on this car.

Find a job, look after myself, find an apartment, a cheap apartment, save my money and find a third-world country, hide out and write for months. Better yet, find the imaginary girl that's been in my mind since I was a boy, a girl I can do everything and anything with. A thousand dollars and a credit card, you never know when an emergency will hit, sometimes one emergency leads to another, so that's why the credit card stays empty of debt, a safety net.

I've found a job.

Muscles repair, the next 100-pound bag is at the end of the conveyor, each bag travelling faster, or is it the dripping sweat and shaking arms that delude my senses. I'm more alert than I've ever been, working a job of three. Each bag rubs my wrist and a rash is set to bleed. I'll continue to look for five extra seconds so I can retrieve a drink of water. I run up the conveyor belt putting myself ahead of the bags; one, two, three bags up will give me ten seconds at my disposal. I find my drink of water. How many hours left, I won't check the clock, I'll pretend it doesn't exist and when six o'clock rings I'll be surprised the day has an end. I hate the job and love the work at an exhausting defeating rate.

A foreman stops my progress, 'Go into my office, some people want to talk to you.'

'Who wants to talk?' I question.

'Cops, detectives,' is the foreman's answer.

'What the fuck!' I spout.

A couple of guys in suit jackets are chatting in the foreman's office.

I dread nothing, my guard down, good behaviour, and look what I get. Introductions and the standard, 'Have a seat. Do you know Penelope Hargrove?' a detective inquires.

Library Girl, 'Yeah, I know her.'

'What was your relationship?'

'Friends, why?'

'You were lovers,' the Detective tells.

'Why, what's going on?'

'Did you ever hit her, or choke her? Do you like rough sex? When was the last time you saw her? Start with the first question, were you and Penelope Hargrove lovers?'

'Where is the good cop?' This brings a bit of a chuckle, some tension breaks. I start to give an account of myself. 'We had sex, she was an experimental girl, she liked strange things. I haven't seen her in a month. She's a young fun girl. I like her. She isn't the type I'd get romantically involved with, in a committed relationship. I'll tell you everything we did sexually if that's what you'd like to hear, but first what's this all about?'

'Penelope has been murdered.'

I drop to one knee with unrecognizable force, 'What?'

'Her body was found in the woods. Death was caused by suffocation.'

'Tell me everything.'

'First, we have some questions for you. We also have a search warrant for your car and home.'

'What are you talking about? Do you think I had something to do with her death?'

'Can we have the keys to your car?'

'The keys are in my locker. I'll retrieve them for you.' Man, I never knew how much she meant to me. Anger invades . . . she found the wrong guy or the wrong ride. I almost have a fit! 'Can you give me some details?'

'Foul play, she had wire burns on her wrist, and several bruises to her ear, cheekbone, upper outer thigh, and buttocks. The cause of death was suffocation.' They continue with more questions and answers. 'We have a statement from one of her confidants that you assaulted her during sex on more than one occasion.'

'Our sex was different. Call it role-playing. Call it kinky. I couldn't see her anymore.'

The detectives look at each other.

'I've worked here the last twenty-three days in a row. I could not have been in two places at once, it's a seven-hour drive. I've worked ten-hour shifts every day. Go check with the timekeeper, that's the first thing you should have done.'

The detectives return in ten minutes. 'It's unusual for someone to work every day.'

The detectives erase my name from the list of suspects.

Lucky Christmas is the day after tomorrow, my boss has let me take Christmas Eve off.

I'm driving the night with Library Girl in my mind . . . we're in this together. Claire's house is our destination.

At five in the morning, I find sleep on the outskirts of the town, not far from where Library Girl's body was found.

I've slept far too late, it's near nine o'clock.

Claire isn't at her office yet. I'll try her house.

At Claire's house, I find the key. I'm an uninvited guest, one never knows what to expect. Seems quiet, I look through her rooms. No references to her boyfriend or evidence he's been around.

Claire arrives home. Her face is shallow, grave and vacant, you'd say she's lost enormous weight if you were only to look at her face, prominent cheekbones and a nose rupturing about her skin. Her body though tells of despair, she hasn't lost weight, she's gained, her usual tight muscles on a thirty-six-year-old frame now inch towards forty-five. In my recollection, her face tells of someone cracking, hallucinations, and misery.

Claire doesn't speak other than hello as she looks for a drink and settles on water; she hasn't looked me in the eye. No hug, no anger, no apology, or laughter. Claire sits across from me and I ask without thought, 'Where's your boyfriend?'

'He broke up with me.'

'What's his name?'

'What does it matter? He's not in my life anymore. Is that what you're here for? If you want to talk about him then you might as well leave right now. I'm sorry, I'm in no condition to talk about it.'

'Did you know Penelope Hargrove?'

'Yeah, small town, I met her briefly, just after you left.'

'Really, did your boyfriend know her?'

'I don't know,' her answer is aggravated. She finds composure, 'he talked to her outside the house, before I spoke to her.'

'You spoke to her, to Penelope?'

'Yeah, here at the house she was looking for a place to rent.'

'Did you show her my old place?'

'I didn't show her anything, I figured she was here for other reasons. You know checking me out for you to see if I was living with anyone. I know how you like to manipulate young impressionable girls. People think you had something to do with her murder or that maybe you did it. I'll bet you thought nobody knew you were sleeping with her? I'd seen you with her, thought maybe you were friends. In a small town it doesn't take long to find the truth though.'

'It's never the truth unless heard from both sides and you along with everyone else know nothing of the truth of our friendship. What about you Claire, did you think I did it?'

'Nope, you're not the type.'

'Tell me Claire, who do you think killed her? What was your boyfriend's name? Tell me the mystery man's name.' I can see the roots of her hair, her hands are clenched, and her teeth grind.

With a release of tension, she spills, 'Philip Mongoli, okay!'

'How can you deny this Claire, he murdered Penelope, didn't he?'

'How would I know?'

'It's a small town, how many people do you know that choke and beat women during sex? Why did he break up with you?'

'He said things were getting out of hand he missed his wife and kids.' She pauses as if messages are being passed to her from above. Her words are mumbled, 'That same day they found her body.'

'Where is he now?'

'I don't know.'

'Is he still in town?'

'Yes.'

'Claire!' Desperate I am, 'Where does he live?'

'Why, what are you going to do? You're going to destroy me.'

Claire's stillness is overtaken by her pace to nowhere, frantic, her body alive, explosive.

'Where does he live Claire? A girl is dead.'

Her movement halts. She stares, demons have taken her. Her voice normal again, 'You don't know that. Maybe it was an accident,' she continues to glare.

'You're unbelievable, I can't help you.' I walk to leave and a sudden thud heeds my progress. I turn; Claire has hit the floor in a wild tantrum, exhausting herself in emotional relief.

'If he did it,' she rises slightly to look at me. I note that she means what she's about to say, 'Kill him, kill him for me. I can't live through this.' She sobs uncontrollably, I'm silent. She sits on her knees in a ball and lifts her head. Her eyes are round balls of fire. 'How could I befriend a killer, what will they think of me? He couldn't have done it? No, no, this is a dream. Go find out, he lives at . . . Kill him! I don't want a trial in my town. Please . . . no trial, no trial. Kill him and walk away I won't tell . . . you know I won't tell.'

Claire is done for. I leave her speaking absurdities to herself, absurdities of truth.

The path is of an angel's, I see Library Girl on every street corner. As I reach the outskirts of town I see her rise with wings and a smile. I look to my right and there she is in my passenger seat, a bit disturbed. She turns and flashes a smile. I blink and find the turn-off to Philip's home. A dirt road on Christmas Eve, no snow yet to cover the pot-holes, the address is scratched out on a post in red paint. A shit-hole, he lives in an old rusted mobile home, a twelve-foot-wide trailer. He has neighbours on either side; with the help of trees his shit-hole isn't totally exposed. It's coming to me now, how could Claire be so stupid, she'd fallen for big talk in nice dress. The guy looked good, but it appears he's skin deep. I peek in the trailer and the dishes aren't done, maybe he'll be back. Garbage bags sit outside; he'll be back. I drive away and find a meal.

What will I do, what to say, playing the scene out in my head, a struggle, a knife, a death? Maybe Claire's right, maybe I'm making a mistake? Not mistaken. Something is hiding in this man, I could feel it the first time I saw him, he bugged the piss out of me, scary. Maybe I've taken hate and placed murder beside hope. I'd dealt Library Girl the gloves that killed her. I want to know why, how this has happened. I'm as involved as any of the participants of this awful incident, it is my trial as well as theirs. Never harm another through speech, philosophy, witnessed acts, or pleasurable games. Yes, my own gain is not worth others' lives. I feel pain and tears of guilt, of wrong, of bad, of a selfish man, a weakling, a coward, and a misbehaved thief, low as life as they come; only one thing to do, find truth. A worn van with horrible curtains coloured insane is now parked in Philip's drive, he's home.

Philip speaks, 'Come in, I know who you are. I was just leaving to go spend Christmas with my children.' Children, they were never in the equation, I guess anyone can have children, somebody's father.

'How long will you be staying?' he asks smiling.

'As long as it takes, tell me about Penelope.'

'She told me all about you, she loved you. Have you seen Claire? I miss her. I like her, you know.' His eyes are dancing. I find him charming – his black hair slicked back, a great physique. He wears fine clothing, but it's not all right, he's too nice. 'You don't mind if I pack, do you?'

'No.' I've let him have his way. He could walk right out, and I mightn't do a thing, get a grip. I'm so amazed; all the goodness of my life is false all flattery is stripped. Time is lonely. In the worst of people, we still look for the best, and in the best, we look for fault. I enjoy this time. It's a peace I haven't suspected.

'What happened?' I ask direct.

'What?' He heard me I don't have to repeat myself.

I explain, 'Penelope, how did you meet Penelope?'

He sits down now on a chesterfield, I'm on a kitchen chair; the living room and kitchen collide. 'I'm bigger than you,' he says with a smile. 'You didn't bring a gun? If I had a gun, I'd shoot myself right now. You didn't bring a gun?'

I'm not shocked by his stance.

'No, no gun.' I continue to play his way, I sniff disgusted.

'No weapon, I'd win if we had a fight, I'm bigger and stronger than you.' I have no answer for the words he's used. He continues, 'I will turn myself in once I visit my kids and well away from town, away from Claire. I want to protect Claire from all this, that's why I broke it off with her, to salvage her reputation. Reputation is everything. I've been in this town for six months, the town before that my reputation was shattered. I guess I have more than a reputation to worry about in this town.' A bizarre laugh proceeds. 'You have a good reputation. Claire spoke highly of you and so did Penelope. Penelope... where do I begin? You didn't call her Penelope, did you? You called her . . . oh I can't remember. Help me, what was it?'

My voice is soft, near absent, 'Library Girl.'

His laughter has now reached hysterics. 'She had sharpness about her . . . Penelope was something you had to possess after one look of her eyes. I'm right . . . Penelope brought strong sexual desire on my shoulders and yours too. She was a must in the catalogue.'

Like a therapist, I sit. 'How did you meet her?'

He obliges, 'She came by Claire's and we talked outside, she claimed to be looking for a rental. She was really looking for me though, an obsessed girl she wanted to be bound and lashed. The little story that you told her about me tying up Claire for the morning while I was out intrigued her. It was lust at first sight. We made a secret arrangement to meet at a house not far from here. It was a new listing, empty. Claire wouldn't have anything to do with the girl, jealousy.' He looks squarely at me, daring me. 'What do you want to know, everything right?' His voice grows loud, commanding, disgruntled. 'She turned role reversal, assaulting me, telling me when to come and when not to come, where to meet, and what time. She liked to slap me. I warned Penelope not to abuse me. She said she couldn't, she told me to strap her hands for my own protection. She really wanted to control me. On the last day I picked her up in my van, she'd go jogging in the woods and I'd pick her up at the edge of the path. I don't know if she ever jogged, but nobody ever saw us meet there. She wanted to be bound in the van. I parked the van and bound her hands with some wire.' He stops in mid-sentence, 'Do you want a drink?'

I softly motion, 'No.'

'The rest is graphic, but I'm sure it's nothing that you haven't seen before, you're not much different from me. You just don't go all the way.' We stare at each other, not in battle but in study. 'Well, she begged me to untie her, I wouldn't though I just laughed and said "now it's my turn to be the aggressor". I'd been very civilized with her up to that point, and I think that's why she was always pissed at me. You know ordering me around, slapping me. Well, I laid a good beating on her, she didn't like it . . . she tried to bite me. I wrapped wire around her neck, but the look on her face was so terrifying, I covered her head with a pillow. She stopped moving after some time.' He smiles in reflection.

I can't think, I'm frozen in thought nothing is real but perfectly complete. I walk to the phone and ask him to call the police.

'It was an accident, you know,' he pleads.

'Phone the police,' I firmly request.

'Let me die, kill me, there's a knife in the drawer.'

'Phone the police.' I order this time in temper, 'Phone the police.'

He dials the number. 'Hi, my name is Philip Mongoli and I have information on the death of Penelope.' He drops the phone.

'Tell them.' I pick up the phone and hold it to his mouth, 'Tell them!'

He's whimpering. 'I killed her by accident,' he speaks to me away from the receiver.

'You murdered her!' I yell and strike him with the receiver of the phone.

Reality and cohesiveness return and I rattle off the address to the dispatcher and yell, 'Hurry!' Any violent act I may have dreamed or stopped myself from performing is vanquished. My body is empty of aggression. I've never felt peace from brutality until today.

I sit and watch a man crumple. Tears spill out of his eyes, his end is near, he cares to go out calmly. 'Penelope was crazy, it's her own fault. Will you kill me now?' he begs me. 'Can you do that for me? I've been good to you. Let me take my own life.' He stands and walks towards the door.

'Where are you going,' I question.

'To die . . . coming?' I follow. He's searching the van, a rope is found, and a tree. He ties the rope in a fashion for strangulation.

'There's a sawhorse in the trailer, can you get it for me?' I do.

The rope is thrown over a strong branch of the tree and a loop awaits his neck. I drop the sawhorse.

'Thank you.' He positions the sawhorse. Something we've all thought, a tragedy at one's own hands. As an eyewitness, it seems not a sin but a gift. Can I let him die? I don't care, die! The loop is over his head, and now the sawhorse must be kicked away. 'Thank you, you're a good man, I'll see you in heaven,' he smiles and releases panic laughter as he kicks over the horse.

Library Girl's parents are what I think, can't stop the thought, haven't met her parents.

I run to the trailer and find the drawer with a knife.

Returning to the scene I jump up on the sawhorse to cut the rope, he drops. He's alive, in a great deal of pain.

Why should I let him have his way? Like Claire and Penelope, I've been charmed. I wish to escape, but it's my responsibility that he be punished awake. 'Kill him, kill him!' voices deep inside me cry.

I wait in my car, a cop car, two cop cars, and many questions.

The police move inside the trailer, and I sneak away. I turn at the intersection of a place where two highways collide. I spy what seems to be a girl with long hair. As I drive close, I'm mistaken, it's a man. I hear Library Girl laugh. Christmas day alone.

© Les Cook

Departure, Flagrant

———

MACAU, THE END OF THE '90s.

I'm in the entrance of a famous hotel casino.

Looking for the nut-ball I've been gallivanting around Asia with.

Where is the paunch belly scam fucker? I left him with a bewitching Thai hooker who hadn't the slightest interest in him. He shouldn't be longer than twenty minutes with her.

My acquaintance goes by many names, I'll call him Alexi. He's been saying he's from everywhere from Afghanistan to the Ukraine.

My head tilts at the sound of my name. It's Alexi.

He sits with umbrella cocktails in the company of a beautiful Chinese girl, twenty-two with wavy burgundy hair.

'She's from Shanghai.' Enthusiastic Alexi, like he's hit the jackpot. 'I met her when I bought a drink. She laughed at me because the servers cannot understand my English. She is a very nice girl.'

Shanghai Girl in heavily accented English, 'Yes I laugh, he is funny, I help him.'

I like her voice, English school or English boyfriend?

Alexi is handsomely demented, astoundingly charming. He is no challenge for Shanghai Girl. I can see she is genuine.

Alexi happily explains his situation, 'I finish with the other girl. She was no good! But this girl is very nice,' an innocent motion, a gesture to Shanghai Girl.

Shanghai Girl clarifies, 'If she didn't satisfy you, you didn't have to pay her. If the girl does not provide what you ask you do not have to pay her.'

'Yes, but we had sex. Therefore, I must pay.' Alexi continues, 'She wouldn't let me touch her. I finish quick, and then we finish. What is that? She does nothing, I can't touch her, and she doesn't kiss. Sure I pay her, but I don't like her. She wasn't naked in bed.'

'Why don't you go with this girl?' I conclude the obvious. 'Will you go with him?' Direct at Shanghai Girl.

'Yes, if he likes, I will go.'

Time isn't wasted, money is to be made and Alexi is to be satisfied. Shanghai Girl politely invites me to come along with the excuse that should I care to meet Alexi in an hour I shall know where to find him. She's clever. Drinks are left a quarter full.

Eighth floor, more girls smile near the elevator, they scuffle across the hall from room to room.

My eyes cavort up Shanghai's leggy steps, an extreme surge of excitement as we near her room. Some of my adrenaline is happy for Alexi, and the rest of my adrenaline up Shanghai's legs.

'Come in for a minute,' she guides us into an impressive two bed room. Another girl lays awake under the sheets.

'She is pretty. She is your roommate?' Alexi questions Shanghai Girl.

'Yes, you like her?' Shanghai answers in question.

'If she likes me, I like her.' Ecstatic he states.

'If you want her, she will take you,' Shanghai Girl relinquishing herself from Alexi.

I thought she was smart, and she's proven she is.

Alexi slips in with Shanghai's friend. 'She likes me. She is pretty like you.'

Shanghai Girl is cool with Alexi's enthusiasm, 'Yes, I don't mind; have her.'

With these words I can't resist Shanghai Girl. From nothing to something, I'd asked for nothing today, but in a sudden moment like a hurricane my hands roam up her legs. She turns. Our mouths spark as we embrace. We balance to her bed. Alexi is engaged in his girl; they are in motion when our lust reaches the bed.

A rubber, thrusting, moaning, rapid pounding, lifting. I have done what I hadn't expected and I like it, I like it a lot, to be a beast again.

Alexi shouts at me, 'Don't hurt her,' again he shouts, 'Don't hurt her! I warn you.' He can hear Shanghai's passion and he can see my ruggedness, 'Don't hurt her.'

We fall to the floor humping, laughter. I withdraw, drink water.

Alexi now stands on his bed in agony, his fingers squeezing the end of his knob, his belly sticking out. Shanghai Girl bewildered at Alexi's posture; he's attempting to delay his mounting spray from spitting out. His shot thwarted; he jumps back onto the girl.

Shanghai Girl pleads, more kisses, a new rubber, and lovers again.

Alexi watches as I lift Shanghai Girl to his bed.

'Oh my god!' speaking frantic is Alexi, 'Not on our bed you have your own bed.' Alexi is snuggled in his girl's breast, now finished his sexual escapade.

Shanghai Girl bursting into laughter, and I into tears. Another sheik is up until the hour done. Alexi's girl gives me a thumb up and a voiced, 'You are good, very good!' I don't know if I'm 'good' I only know it has been that long. I'm out of breath and extremely euphoric. Shanghai hasn't asked for money, yet. I leave her more than her friend has negotiated with Alexi.

Shanghai speaks, 'Thank you, I hope to see you again.' She passes me her mobile number. I pass the number to Alexi to jot down.

We walk as proud peacocks, smiling and gifted.

Alexi excited, 'I have never seen a man like you with such hunger. You are very strong. You take a drug?'

'No,' I respond.

'Be honest with me. I have seen no man fuck as you without a drug. You are an incredible man. I've never seen a man like you. You must teach me.'

'No drugs, just the right girl.'

'I like Russian girls. I speak their tongue. Then you will see. You will be surprised,' Alexi claims. I believe him.

'In the night the Russians come out.' I advise.

'Then in the night, you will see me in action, you will be impressed. I have the tongue for the Russian language, you will see and you will be surprised. This Chinese girl is okay, but she doesn't kiss. She is not like Shanghai Girl, Shanghai Girl is very nice, she has very nice breasts. You were a very lucky man today and I too. We are kings.'

I wish that money was just a gift, to be used as pleased.

Once you commit to something you have to follow true no matter how cruel.

A monster in a whore maze, Alexi fucks along. 'I can't fuck anymore, nothing comes out. I must rest, no more girls for two days.'

He'll be fucking again the next day.

'I fuck her, she tells me to stop. I was hurting her. Like you, I fuck her very well! Women don't like a big cock. They say they do but they don't; they like a small cock. I fuck for one hour she was very sore. A man shouldn't fuck every day, he needs to take breaks. Fucking every day will kill a man.'

'You call the Romanian girl?' I question him.

'Yes, I call her late last night.'

'Fuck her?'

'I don't want to see her again, ever. She doesn't love me. I don't love the Romanian. Never will I love her. I will not give her the satisfaction of my love.'

'Don't call her again, find the Nordic girl. She likes you, not your money; she kisses you. The Romanian may be the best, but she isn't the best for you.'

'She is the worst. I never want to see her again.'

He smiles happily in his filthy dilemma.

'I will call the Romanian now.'

He is a savage beast, a stupid animal, I love it.

'You just said you never want to see her again.'

'Yes, but I want one last time with her. I will call her now.'

'She'll be sleeping.'

He calls. He must move on to what he thinks in the morning to plan his day. Continued calls until she turns off her phone, he laughs stunned, 'She has turned off her phone, she sleeps now.'

I make my own call.

My eyes open her lashes' flap, as does her tongue on my upper lip, a different kiss, but fucking in a familiar motion.

Shanghai Girl speaks holding me in stride, 'I want to stay the night here, but my boss will be mad. In the morning my boss sleeps, I can see you then. My boss doesn't let me be free. I have to give him money all the time. When I saw you talking with the Russian girls, I was a little upset... jealous. I knew then that I liked you more than I should.'

'Is that why you kiss me or do you always kiss men?'

'No, I never kiss a man. Sometimes a girl gets excited and she kisses. Your friend Alexi is mad that the girl didn't kiss him. Girls don't have to kiss the man. We aren't paid to kiss. Most girls won't kiss and don't kiss,' she explains.

'How many men have you kissed while working?'

'Two, the other man I kissed from Hong Kong. You know my boss has lots of power in Macau. All my money goes to my boss and my mother. In a month I won't have to give money to my boss. I can save all my money for my mother in Shanghai. I do this for my mother so she can keep her house. I only know the discos and the hotel I stay in Macau. I don't know the sunlit streets well.'

Alexi and I go for coffee one last time.

Alexi will take the fast ferry to Hong Kong tonight and fly back to where he came from. 'This was the best time of my life, the best!' Alexi speaks.

He takes one last spin, unable to walk, unable to come, but he has fun, he leaves all his money spent with a large grin. 'I dance so much I can't walk. I have a pain in my gut, too much sex. I will never forget Macau. This is the best I've ever lived!'

My mind has stopped listening to him. I have to go home soon.

The last thing Alexi said to me was, 'I think you never have a problem.'

True; I thought in the scale of all in life.

Scorched is the way I see the life of people. We can pretend to be good, even humanize it – but in the end, we are all the same – we slowly or quickly destroy everything in our path. Some people call it survival of the fittest but when we study the human body, we call it disease when something comes to the forefront and takes over.

British Columbia.

My vacation hasn't ended just because I'm home. The vacation has followed me home.

Television; drinking five cups of tea, driving my car for miles, turning around for more tin foil to heat so I can smoke my burden away.

Indeed, I'm weak, I must dream.

Even pussy has infiltrated my mind.

The return from vacation – I can't pretend I'm happy. Like my life a plastic front that speaks okay, though inside is complications that can't be understood; it is this front that will let the false explanation of life be understood.

Superstition

One more trip and I'll be okay.

I wish South America to numb my mind of life, fuck, and smoke.

I fly to South America.

I fuck my brains to a sense of stabilization.

Now I have rhythm, reason, the holiday to South America was needed to concede my life has been lived well so I can die without regret.

Fear is gone. Desire is gone. I can die. I can live.

I am confident; I've followed the superstition script. The urge for satisfaction is dead, I'm alive. I've satisfied my life, and only love waits, but love can wait, can wait forever if need be. There was a time when the thought of fuck took over; one last fuck ruled; that time has passed, success at nothing now rules my mind.

Expect everything from a holiday.

I remain content for some time.

The difference between defeat and win is slim.

I gamble and return to Macau.

⚓

© Les Cook

Ecstatic

TRIPFIENA

I think I'm principled.

I first recognized this disease in my mother. Passed on, it has grown stronger with nourishment in me.

My disease has become dormant of late. I've become civilized as I've decided to travel to Eastern Russia – Vladivostok.

I go to finish my life, die in the cold.

It is similar to where I was born.

I don't want to die where I was born, similar is good, satisfied in death, not secure.

I'm past thirty-four years of age.

Mongolia is my rest before my final escape to Russia.

There is a dormitory of a small school where I can sleep and eat. The school offers courses on Mongolian culture.

The school is closed for a week. The caretaker of the school takes some of my money and delivers a bed in a spacious room among seven other beds. Two students leave the room with packed bags as I enter. No words are spoken. The dormitory has four toilets, four showers, lockers, and a very large sink for washing.

I have use of a kitchen.

A woman rests reading a book on a bed two away from the bed I've chosen. She has extraordinary looks, fascinating. So fascinating, I cannot stare. She only nods in recognition of me. The small commotion of comings and goings does not grant a proper greeting between us.

Still the fascinating woman reads her book as I sort my things.

Will she ever speak?

The book she reads appears to be Russian.

I haven't a book, I have nothing, not a notion of what to do, but explore.

'Going for a walk?' she exclaims.

Stop, look, react, 'I don't know, I guess a walk. Look around.'

'There is a nice walk, not long, it goes to a park and you have leisure amongst a few trees. Is this what you are looking for?' she asks.

'Yes, sounds nice.'

'There is food and drink near the park. It isn't too cold outside now.'

'Where?' I ask.

She takes my words. 'Can I show you? I wouldn't mind some food and sun. Let me change – you can wait outside.'

I want to say 'yes' as polite and as intelligent as she, I know the words but I just nod.

Lunch isn't supposed to bother me, I know I will eat little and this will satisfy my appetite. In her presence what is one to eat? How can a man chew savagely?

Plotting... what is my story for her, the cheapest one-night room in town?

Should I guess where she's from and not say a word?

She sounds Canadian but speaks like she's been in Russia a long time.

At the park, we have soup.

'I studied literature in Canada for four years,' she says.

Literature, it would have to be literature. Isn't one to study literature in Russia and travel to Canada? I prefer her way. If one is to study literature you may like to live as if you are the ones in the books, or as the ones who wrote the books. I've waited all my life to find a woman who studied literature. Is it too late now?

She says she's a Russian girl. She may have Russian blood – but I doubt she is Russian. Clearly, even with a somewhat Russian accent she is as much a Canadian as my sister is. I don't pry. I will let her be what her mind likes and what she portrays.

All the smartness that I once thought has sunk. It is like she has bitten my neck sharply and my blood has begun to drain. I must think clearly or it will be perceived that my livelihood has been sucked dry.

I can't escape pulse.

I can escape conversation.

Pulse is king, not speech. We all can't speak.

Can I justify speech and once I've heard all she says, can I then wait each day for her pulse to beat to mine?

It seems hours upon hours that we, sit, walk, talk, eat, and drink in the park before we relax in the dormitory. I don't recall another conversation as intimate as the conversation we've had and yet revealed little of our personal lives.

I can see that her claiming to be Russian will be the story and Mongolia will be the place. A noble setting – a grand event for life or death – it will be one or the other that succeeds.

She sneezes and I grab a tissue. I wanted a cold, I wanted her to have a cold in the dream of this life I was to lead. She smokes and I hate smoke. Her hair is what most gets me. Silly, how hair can get me – how can hair play such an important role? Her hair is plain brown. Her hair doesn't reach her breasts, it is an instant stop. Hair and then breasts is how the eyes greet her. I haven't seen the rest of her yet, a long skirt doesn't fit like slacks or jeans do. Skirts, good, bad, or indifferent, I haven't a feel yet. Sure, she is to be thin, but one always wonders how clean she will be. How about if she didn't have great hair – it doesn't work that way – she has sexy hair and it is what she uses, a part of her personality that she thrusts forward. When she talks, I look at her face and slowly focus on her words, her eyes, and soon I believe all she says and the passion she projects. Once past her hair you meander in the slow movements and motion she claims; soon you want to move slow, talk low. One shouldn't act as a fool or a child in her room. One should only speak a few select words and try not to think too much.

I move about now as dusk descends, ordering my space around and how my things should be placed. She doesn't read, she watches me and fiddles with clever words and strict flirtation. I can't touch as quickly as she flirts, she's hidden her flirtation with kindness and I've done the same. Unable to exploit the opportunity, I walk to prepare a shower. Her eyes, they follow me, still as a flirt.

Ripping my clothing and fucking me with her eyes.

Am I scared?

No, not scared; cautious of a girl as this – cautious she is playing, or worse, she is not.

———————

MY BRAIN IN THE MORNING sees things differently. It has only been in the last few months that I've noticed this trickery. What triggered this knowledge is when I'd read e-mails in the morning. I'd read the e-mails later in the day or the following day and everything that I thought the e-mail said was totally different than what I'd grasped in the morning. This false information is the failure of my life. I wonder what else I will see backwards? When I'm in my final days, will I suddenly notice that I haven't seen anything correctly?

So do I see her correctly this morning, my roommate you could say, do I really enjoy the looks, the oddity of my roommate?

My imagination is tempted.

A better look today – only a towel wrapped around her lean body.

She's spoken of taking a walk outside but her towel hasn't left her body. She's showered, dried, and applied another dry towel and panties. Still, she doesn't dress, just relaxes on her bed.

'You have many white towels,' I remark.

I've witnessed her go through three white towels today.

'Do you want one? I have many. I found them in the laundry room.'

'Yes.' I answer.

She reaches under her bed and finds a white towel. She extends her arms towards me with a towel laid across her forearms. I walk to her bed for the towel. With the length of her body now flat on her bed the towel wrapped around her body doesn't reach to cover her underwear. I move slowly, looking furiously at her panties. They are tight white – full rounded are the cheeks her panties hold, not flat. With both hands, I reach for the towel that lay across her forearms. Her hands slide to my hands and the towel falls from her forearms to the floor.

Our touch is sensual in unison – my body gravitates to be with her body.

My hands are released and search her back.

In a motion of beauty, she rolls to her hip.

My hip is now on her bed.

Erection has come quick.

I'm not afraid. She wets my trousers with a tongue of saliva and unbuttons my pants. My full cock is direct in her mouth – my mouth targets her panties. I haven't removed her panties, they are clean, gorgeous. I stroke, taste, and stretch them.

We could continue our position as it is now for hours.

The position is one of experience, not animalism.

She has removed her panties and towel.

My clothing is removed.

She stops engulfing my cock, turns her body. She's knelt forward and I've entered her. Soon she lands her hands on the floor. I walk her, my full length inside her to my bed where one hand at a time she climbs onto. She rotates her body so we can face each other for the first time in finale. We don't stop, we rock as a cradle. For the first time we are kissing, I can't stand it – we are making love, the acrobatics are gone, our eyes open.

All we talked yesterday and revealed nothing but that our hearts needed healing and our organs spat for sex.

Have sex.

Fall in love.

Ask questions.

Is this how to keep sparks lit long enough to suggest a lasting relationship is best? So fast, so sudden, I hadn't expected this – I lie though, I expected something.

"Why do you go to Russia?" she asks as the sun has settled and the sex surely done.

I answer in somewhat truth, 'I wrote a book, everything that I thought I'd put in the book I didn't end up putting, so now I'll write another.'

'You've left everything behind to accomplish what you thought you already had but hadn't?'

'Yes, I've come to give up the grievance of wealth, the grievance of pussy. To truly be happy I've given up so I can find health, love, and death. I've come to die. My life is displeasure. My last resort is to travel here and write a story of fear. Madness – we live until we destroy, we destroy our own existence. I'm ready for death. I'm ready to go elsewhere.'

'Mars?' she hints.

'No,' I laugh.

She is poetry; this is why she is rested on a bed next to mine in an uncommon setting.

I'VE MADE LOVE TO HER, now I want intimacy.

She pretends she's Russian but I don't even think her blood is Russian. If I'm to believe the words she speaks, she is a Russian visiting Mongolia. And going... I don't know where she is going.

'My name is Tripfiena,' she confides. "Trip, fiend, take away the d and add a. Trip-fiend-a. Tripfiena. Do you like?'

I think she's told me another lie but really if she likes her name to be Tripfiena, then Tripfiena she will be.

She leaves mystery exactly where it bounded on my cock and now stands.

'I will tell you now, I'm Russian. I have Russian blood as you guessed, though you didn't say it, you guessed that I'm the same as you. I'm born and raised Canadian. I have lived well in Russia. I've spent six years off and on in Russia. I like to think I'm Russian, it is part of my show. I make money performing my show. Now I will tell you why I claim as my blood and not my culture. You can like me or hate me – but I will tell you now that I am clean – I don't have a disease – and I'm not a slut. I learned that for me to live as I like I need money and freedom to move around and do as I like. It is my escape, when I'm Russian I sleep with men for money. I study in Russia as a Canadian student and I travel to the South of Asia as a freelance Russian prostitute. I don't work in a brothel nor do I sleep with every man I meet. I play a game with a man I like but don't love, the man who likes fucking but won't settle to love, though begs it. It is the best seduction tool when you don't love but like. I give the man what he wants, sex if they must. I receive money from men without sex occasionally. I've seen some men for years. Lonely aching hearts I win. Shattered hearts when they figure that I lie, they all figure it out in time and if they figure it out first, they love it. Men are the same as women, they try to change the bad into good, but one cannot buy a good heart that they'd bought as a bad heart. Men hate me or love me – but they always pay me.'

Congratulations.

I find her story too amazing.

I like what I've heard, her own invention her hidden identity to the world, a Russian woman working South Asia. An American, a Taiwanese, a Frenchman, and Japanese if I'm to believe these four men were the only men she slept with last year. She said these four gave her enough money to travel, study, and live for the year.

The Eastern people vie for a chance to live in the West and she comes to the East to live like them. She has experience without sinking, only sinking in. It is amazing her story, told so direct.

Tripfiena, I don't have to ask why you thought of this name.

We've spent the day in the dormitory – we've bought food and cooked in the kitchen, read books, and made love. By night she asks what I've expected her to do.

'No job, no children, no special someone you've been thinking of?' she asks.

'No, just write, fuck, eat, drink, die,' I answer her.

'Well, you've fucked me, we ate, you wrote a little this morning so tonight we will drink. You only have one thing left after we fuck again.' She pauses, 'Death.'

'Suppose so.'

'You want to die by your own hands?' she questions me.

'Unless I'm unlucky.' I stop and reflect before I begin to speak again. 'At a time, I wanted to die sweet at the edge of sex in the arms of a woman. This is when I was scared of death. I can't expect my lover to do the same, but I can offer her the means. My death at the edge of an orgasm, a double death looking into our eyes the last time.'

'How?' Tripfiena asks.

'Self-inflicted, I guess. A drug plunged into my vein or swallowed from my lover's mouth.'

She hesitates, 'You're not suicidal, are you?'

'No, I'm mad at the world. The world stole me of life! My mind isn't free, my mind is too free, my mind is killing me with indecision. Torture – this is why some societies can survive and even thrive better in dictatorship than freedom.'

'You don't have freedom because your mind owns you. You're lost so you go to Russia to find and if you don't find, you die. Correct?'

'Correct.' I answer. 'Too much freedom is no good. You must be free with reason, without reason a man can't be free, nature won't let him. Rules and following them are starting to make sense to me because I have freedom and I'm crazy about what to do with it.'

'And do you have a broken heart as well?'

It is the question that was to be asked yesterday after we made love or before we made love. It is asked now though, and I've had time to think.

'I don't know. I have or had a fiancée. It was a short brilliant engagement. I loved the ring on my finger, simply loved the twisted gold. I hoped someone would look, ask. I never got over the fact that another human that I loved could love me back the same. After her, I wanted to give up on women. I'm incapable of handling what I so deeply desire. I don't want to be crushed.'

'Maybe you should go for the right girl,' is Tripfiena's answer.

'She was the right girl. I can't go backwards.'

'So, go forward.'

'Good answer, forward instead of death, I like this idea.'

'It is a simple idea, but you want complex, dramatic. What happened to your fiancée?'

'Nothing – I killed the relationship. I left, never saw her again.'

'You're not speaking the truth.'

'Like you, I'm speaking my truth, the truth I want to preserve.'

'Are you rich? I don't think you're rich. You wouldn't stay here if you were, but isn't it the rich who want to die? The poor want to survive until they get rich.'

'I have nothing!'

Tripfiena rants, 'You have your mind – it isn't enough for you – you're simple, is this it?'

'If I was simple – I'd be fine with my mind.'

I don't want to reminisce about the past, born today and learn today. The past has been learnt and shouldn't be sought. But it is the past that has brought me here – the world screwed me of my good beliefs. As much as I'd like and want to fuck the world back, I can't. I've lost, lost to rip off the humans of the world as I've been ripped. I guess I did believe those religious texts – written to save.

———

CAN I DEEM MYSELF A monkey, a sailor, a failure?

Hope is all I can promise, even in my wildest dreams money isn't at the end of my ambitious rope. Poetry has never won happiness. Happy sometimes for the reader but for the writer it is to forget unhappiness. Why would one write if they were happy? Tell me what the need is other than money and pure enjoyment. Well, money isn't a reason and enjoyment isn't a necessity.

Tripfiena hasn't a goal and it is the answer, no agenda, no ladder, and therefore no strict code. She is free. I'm a mere shadow of what she sees. I see nothing but what is the greatest a man should and could be though I haven't the knowledge to get it but to cheat.

You don't get to be a prophet it just comes and to whom it has come they have fought their beliefs. I'm dreaming of becoming what I hate and thus I'm not succeeding.

I was told to be it, to be greatness, told inside my head, and I'm being told Tripfiena is greatness. It is always like this when you newly meet one that you like – you only see greatness. Still, it is her silence that keeps any thought of leaving her behind soon far away.

She does speak of a past, all brief half stories, always letting me wonder what is, what was the full story. If I pry, her quietness sulks and our friendliness will become distant.

It is as we eat dinner in the dormitory that I speak as always. It was the first day that I met her that I couldn't speak. Since making love, I love to speak to her in brief bursts. We are politicians, diplomats, antagonists, cons, and most of all we want to look good to our lover.

How long was I engaged usually comes next but it hasn't come up, Tripfiena hasn't asked these questions.

She says instead, 'You've come here to die, and I've come here to live. What are we going to do about this problem? I die with you or you live with me? I've never been so sad.'

She, the Russian girl, is so consoling.

She is exactly what I've asked – more proof of my burden – a Russian whore, but she isn't a Russian whore, she's a Canadian actress.

Die with me sunshine, let you rest on my bed, let me wake on our bed.

Tripfiena doesn't stop her triumphant skilled perusing rhythm. 'You must be sad with me or I shall not be happy with you.'

True.

Too kind, true to her disobedience true to her appeal, true to her detachment, true that if she doesn't speak as such, no fool will attempt to save her.

It is almost an embarrassment that I'm the one who wants to die and she the one who wants to live.

'You'll be sad with me and I'll be happy with you,' is my answer.

'Why?' She's asked the question why I'm to be happy and she sad.

I won't answer her question. I won't let her or any woman know that I can't, I can't give love, only take it, die with it.

Sure we are slow, methodical – our seclusion in vastness makes for quickness in closeness. We have discussed what to do when the dormitory is full in a few days. I don't want to see it gone, I don't want to see the dormitory gone but gone like everything as I look to the sky and what do I see? Stars long gone by, I see nothing but the past. What are we to speculate when our roof top is a view of years eons long past? The future has been answered and I can't see it. Stars gone life gone. Life has already past, the future already seen, is this why I know Tripfiena is the one who doesn't want to live and I'm the one who does?

———————————

ON TWO BEDS ACROSS from each other we lie.

She asks what I have never told anyone.

'I'll ask you now, why don't you have money? Did you once have? You have a way about you – a way that tells me you aren't just poor.'

'I gambled. Invested with a friend. I couldn't stop myself; the lure of money was too great.'

'You're not giving me the whole picture.'

'Some stories shouldn't be told, no matter how exciting, interesting, legal, illegal, or in-between.'

'But you are not a criminal.'

'No, but my friend is.'

'Friends, quick friends are like this.'

'I was tempted to kill him but I didn't. A baseball bat to the leg, a foot to the head, or just forget it, never mind about it – my mistake. He lost too. It wasn't only the idea of making money; it was a friendship, a lifestyle I had a weakness for. The first time I made money, travelled, partied, had the time of my life, after that I chased, falling deeper, and deeper in debt trying to capture the feeling again.

'You couldn't walk away, could you?'

'No.' I answer.

'Deep inside you knew you may get screwed. You dreamed of the smile when you first found success. You persisted because you thought you could change the momentum, alter the occasion. You were mad – you thought you couldn't lose, you thought you were invincible. Making the mistake of thinking as a human – I won't say "child" because if you thought as a child you'd shy away, but you thought as a kid. Are you now an adult?'

'Yes – I expect I don't have to wait till I'm old for my money to be spent.'

'Don't let this happen again, don't be fooled by a good feeling.'

SOMEHOW, SOMEWHERE I want to get up there and die, kill the monster. I know I'll find another, but one death at a time. Whatever disease has come along there will be a percentage of people who though exposed to a deadly disease will never suffer from it. I believe I'm one of these people that hold life in their hands. No one likes to hear what I say but it is true that some people are already immune.

It is certain now that I bluntly speak what is on my mind.

'I was a lucky man, women loved to pleasure me in unexpected places, in sensual exploring ways.'

Tripfiena flatters, 'You have a great ass – the kind women love to eat – that sort of woman will do all she can to feast on you. And that is all there is to it – a good face, a large cock, and a great ass. The most important thing is recognizing the woman who will exploit these features to the highest erotic degree. Have you done this? Have women satisfied your dirtiest, most pleasing, and unique dreams? If they have then you are ready for a woman like me. Do you recognize these things I've spoken in me?'

'I've done many things. What else can you add?'

'I can't add a thing. This is why you're ready for me – you will accept me as I am and not what you lust.'

'I haven't a cent.'

'That is what love is – naked. Some people make love with their clothes on – some people use money, and others use placement, status, race, comfort. I make love naked – love is all, it hasn't place, it hasn't status. Tribes, religions, villages have all done the opposite. The powerful have flaunted love to be engaged in rules and tradition and thus love is no longer love, but issued. If I'm the leader of a tribe and I love someone and that someone wants to love another I'll set out rules so I'm not hurt. It is all to do with power, family, and serving. All to do with what making love isn't. Love and making love are two different things – love stops others from making love.'

'You've gone round in a circle. I'm beginning to understand why there are rules to making love and falling in love.'

'Sorry – anarchy – fuck who we want when we want – it would be nice but the human race just isn't that intelligent. If you are intelligent, you'll make love to whom you love no matter what the consequence and, or, gossip.'

Do her words tell me to make love to her without thought, only lust?

'I understand,' is my answer.

She asks, 'Can you do this, let go of your world that surrounds you and love?'

'I don't know.'

'Let me know when you know.'

Where will I find myself in a year is what I want to know. Where will I find myself in a few days when the dormitory is full? I love my life now; I haven't thought and don't want to think. Tripfiena takes care of my future thoughts.

She starts with, 'I will dye my hair blonde soon – a trick for the stupid man, the desperate, the lonely, the thrilling, the exciting, the dying, and most of all the happy-to-spend money man. I will dye my hair blonde soon.'

Am I supposed to question this – save her?

Again, she speaks, 'You say you want to die, but where do you want to live, with your fiancée again?'

'I promised my fiancée the world, and then the truth came out that I could not deliver the world. I am the deceiver?'

'Only in your mind. Women don't care about a long story you told during courtship, just don't tell stories when you've committed. A truth told now can resolve an untold lark of the past.'

————————

LOVEMAKING WITH TRIPFIENA is naked – done without thought as the irresponsible would. I believe Tripfiena doesn't have feelings – is this too strange or is it a perfect position?

It is true now that Russia seems distant and my death impossible.

We haven't an answer to our future.

Tripfiena South, I North, how about together?

What about money?

Will she sleep with other men if I follow her South?

Tripfiena has a bank account, collecting money, so she tells me.

'I love making money, I do nothing and it collects, men are a wonderful money-making tool,' she laughs as she speaks.

It is encouraging seeing her in a white sheet, washed from a shower with no intention to dress for the day. We haven't had lunch. Will she finally dress?

Tripfiena has a vodka concoction ready for consumption, one glass for me and one glass half-finished for her.

'Last night you didn't make love to me. Now we will drink and then make love.' She shouts, 'Drink!'

The sheet is removed.

'Come here.' She talks rough.

I've been told to drink my drink.

I drink my entire drink.

We begin to make love.

She is slow on my chest, talking dreams of what we'll be – travel, study, and then she'll teach me how to make money.

Her message has ended.

My eyes seem to collapse, pulsate.

I've begun to blur.

She is slow above me, riding what I consider an invincible hard-on.

She's done all the work, and the vodka has made me stiff and somewhat incoherent.

It is quite sensational.

I only have to look at her riding me slowly in high ecstasy as she mumbles words (half in Russian) that I plainly don't understand.

'Meet me in the South,' I can understand.

I'll answer yes to anything she says; only I'm fading fast, not to orgasm or even to lose my stiffness, but to keep my vision and hearing in a state of steady function.

'Have this,' she says, 'you want to die? Today you will die – as you come.'

She pumps me faster, harder.

I feel my imploring orgasm may kill me.

I want to die as she's suggested.

It is now that I know that my truest breath of what alive is, is taken now.

I ask myself, what is creature?

I see a short dagger clasped between her fingers.

Like an ice pick tenderly in and out of my chest.

I feel the dagger against, then bounce off my rib.

I can see an insignificant amount of blood on the dagger on my chest.

A culminating orgasm comes.

I close my eyes in a blind extravaganza.

Not certain as I open my eyes in what seems a minute of ejaculation if what I see is true.

The room is quiet.

No sound.

I hear silence, not a horn, not a heart – a cat screeches – a man yells and the dogs sound song.

Tripfiena is gone.

The small dagger that had been between her fingers and into my chest is gone too.

I feel wounded pain, I'm sick with thoughts.

The dreaded 'what if'?

I don't care to move, just – dream.

———————

CIRCUMSTANCES

Vientiane, Laos.

My fiancée's name is Monik.

She is not Muslim, she is not Christian – she is some mixture of Nature, Spirits, Folk, Ghost, and Buddhism.

I've gone too deep with her. I'd like to think the house in the country is a dream.

Not knowing if my fiancée is happy, she waits for my arrival.

I've been away from Monik for five days. A week of truth.

I've been away to meet my business partner, my friend, he didn't show up or correspond.

It is nothing new coming back to Monik after days or even weeks apart. This time it was to be different, payday seemed inevitable, a life together seemed destined. I'd come to collect. The facts are now clear – no love, no money, no future.

No e-mail, no phone call, no show, and now no guessing, my investment lost. That time is gone now, will be a distant memory of a friendship gone wrong. Money can always be regained. Friendships once lost are supposed to be gone. Sometimes you lose on purpose to bust up a friendship that has gone on too long. I'd had faith I'd win. Faith isn't reasoning. I didn't reason, I gambled.

Last night I did everything wrong, and right.

I did what I wanted to do. Be free, a free fool.

I spent the night with another woman, the second woman as in many nights.

I didn't want orgasm last night.

I'd hoped for some kissing, but kissing this girl was difficult. It was the lack of kissing that captured me. Her ass sweet enough for the tip of my cock to rest thirty seconds before I came the first time. This would have been enough I'd be able to get away with this, say goodnight and sleep, innocence obtained.

We were gentle for twenty minutes.

Twenty-five minutes and the attention of my hard cock crammed against her panties penetrated her restricted brain to her throbbing lips. To my surprise innocence was shed, she tore off her panties. Unpredictably she took my cock and placed it into her pussy without a condom, this time the kissing was intimate, she and I wouldn't tease this time. I wanted a full intense explosion inside her wet comfortably wrapped-around-my-knob pussy.

Thankfully I didn't stop it. Hell, I wanted to continue a third time – oh, but the time – my flight!

Last night I did what I'd waited for, wanted.

I felt invincible last night, and this morning awful.

I've arrived early at the airport so as not to miss my flight.

Be sure Monik worries, her father has told her stories of the nightlife in Vientiane, and she has also been a witness. I've kept Monik hidden from events, bewildered. I told her I was going away for business, she accepted this quietly.

What business? She must wonder.

She'd become short with my ill-mannered temper, my constant swearing, my stress exploding for unapparent reasons. Monik had no answer other than I must be unhappy with her. More than unhappy, my health, my heart aching to uncomfortable beats.

'He is always happy, every day,' is how Monik spoke to friends when they asked why she'd fallen in love with me.

Happy has shattered, kind words only arise when I apologize for misguided abuse.

If she finds another man for kindness – I will understand.

As I step to the airplane, I'm close enough to forfeit and walk off; I can't possibly rejuvenate myself with a half-hour of sleep. But I will.

I'll do my best. No excuse of drinking, not sleeping or 'I'm sick' routine, no lies to her, I'll fuck her like the angel I'm expected to be. My legs will give me away, aching after fucking for many days. She'll be sure to look long and hard at my cock – examine it – and ride it until my legs have a pain that rushes down my feet, leaving me unable to sleep.

Booze, sure I could blame booze – but I won't. I was dying to try another pair of legs. It really is an urge as the result of love, a test to thy self, a compliment to her as to say yes to love. This excuse works for me today.

I also know I've come back to her without any money, none. Worse than none, in debt without a thing to look at, in debt not because of a house or car or even a vacation, in debt because of a gamble, an impossible investment to save face from an already impending debt.

At first, Monik doesn't search my cock, she doesn't look for it, she does not even threaten to eat it, but she does promise to. I can wait. I can stall till evening, but I don't, I initiate, proving what she hasn't asked to prove.

Why hasn't she come across to fuck me soundly?

She has fucked with a lack of expression. Does she have guilt?

It is the end of us. One trip too many – or instinct – she hasn't passion as before.

———————————

BORN OF EARTH TO STUDY them (humans) – I'm not really one of them, the theory a constant reminder when I reflect on what my life is.

Monik speaks honestly, 'I'd lie if I said I didn't like cock. Not just any cock – if I liked any cock I'd take cock all day. I'd be rich, money coming in from all four corners of the globe, money rushing to my head. Fuck, and money, and soon I'd choose the cock I'd take, and take it all the way to the bank, and not to this moderate house countryside because I like your cock too much, I've settled as you have.'

What words Monik can pronounce – what a put down, what a compliment!

Monik resolves, 'You never know what foreigner really does, the foreigner have money – that is all, that is all that matters.'

There are always two kinds – a great girl or a great fuck, never one in the same but this twenty-three-year-old girl named Monik with long V-shaped legs was both one in one. I could walk down the street with her smiling and disgust woman and man, make them envy our eroticism. Yet she maintained a certain stature of a woman who was waiting to marry. Splashing my face day after day in her wetness, this is all I thought. I laugh at myself, my stupidity.

Who needs a house? I only need a shack in the countryside, slurping her luscious gash.

Don't give this brief encounter a second thought, take her now, steal her, speak the words 'forever now', and don't worry about the world, just my hunger, her happiness.

Crazy!

I lonely, blind, horny, insatiable – ten minutes of sex that stowed me away.

'You pushed me,' she'd say.

I admitted I didn't like her one hundred percent. Still, deep inside, she knew I loved her.

BROKE IS HAPPY ROMANTIC. Debt is the dangerous place but broke is the exciting place where anything can happen.

I didn't predict my heart would malfunction – something, maybe my kidneys, but my heart? How fast stress can age. My devoured insides, my chest full of pain.

Classic Monik, 'Well, you said money wasn't a problem.'

But increasingly money has become more, and more of a problem than I can solve or talk about.

Yesterday Monik said, 'You don't understand I'm happy with nothing, a roof, food, coffee, freedom of my day. I never asked for money, you just said you had and did provide up until the last two months. You've been grouchy, complaints of spending on this and that and always on things I haven't asked.'

And today – she's spoken, 'You've taken me to the countryside. I never had to steal your money you just gave. Now will I have to steal? I shouldn't say this – I thought I hadn't worries with you – but now I have more than ever.'

I want to speak or ask if she wants me to leave.

I know my answer, I want to leave, run away.

Monik's ass, tits, and magic have slowly become not so impressive.

Her face has become just a face. When we fuck I can no longer attain a pleasurable lasting erection. It is Monik's face, hands, and mouth, but someone else in my mind. I've even shouted other women's names sometimes loud sometimes soft, but always on my lips. I say not an affair, but like it used to be when I was single. Brief romances, and sensational encounters.

Monik speaks what I hope.

'Fuck me, you do that but I'm sick of it. I'd like to go out and have a strange man look at me, touch me. It isn't to get fucked, but the man paying attention to me.'

We are the same.

I say, 'I can leave?'

'If you want, if this is what you like? No problem for me, I can stay alone.'

'I can leave tomorrow.'

'Up to you.' She's reverted back to her native ways.

Whether there will be flowers on the farm this year or next I don't know. I may never know. A month ago, I wondered what I was doing in some simple life and now it is all I wished to have. Again, it is what I've lost.

I've left her with only some of my remaining funds – the majority I've taken with me to fulfill a goal.

I was never one with her. I'm one she's two.

A MILLION STORIES AS this, a foreign man and native woman but not the same, not the same as mine and her story. Again, every man thinks this. Yes, I suppose every story is somehow the same. Just once I wanted to act on thought. To take a girl away without thought, with natural intuition, I've done it and it didn't work without a plan.

Love isn't true, business is true.

I've been away from Monik thirty-three days.

The first thing I did that day when I left Monik is smoke Tiger.

Tiger is a narcotic. I call it Tiger because it takes a bite out of life.

Like many things in life, I didn't like Tiger so much. I didn't think much of it when life was beautiful. Then I tried Tiger when life wasn't beautiful. Tiger made the hours seem like beauty.

At least when my business partner lost my money he gave me something to protect my feelings (Tiger). He knew how much pain I'd be in. Or was it the final appeal to destroy me, the long difficult bullet instead of sudden death.

Tiger vanquished Monik from my brain.

I haven't been aroused in weeks.

I haven't motivation to fantasize – well, I could say I fantasize without the climax or even the buildup. It is nice to sleep without the constant thought of fuck pussy, eat snatch, lick tits, kiss lips.

Tiger can be so calming, looking out the window, listening to music, watching television, and the forgotten cup of tea is lovely.

I negotiated to smoke Tiger and feel good all day, every day.

My brain though began to disintegrate.

I can't do what I want without thought – like my engagement to Monik. This is why engagement became so desperate. I wanted it though I wasn't ready for engagement, another adventure called too loud – I just needed a fuck up to make it a sound decision.

A week ago, I bought an airplane ticket from China where I sit now, to Mongolia, where I will sit tomorrow.

After I bought the ticket, I threw away my bag of Tiger unable to quit on my own.

When you quit smoking Tiger – all the answers of life are asked and answered in a plain, painful way. Answers that you never want to hear, you never want to admit. I'm not God. I spent two days crying about what I've done to my life and before these two days I spent three days with bones of pain screaming nerves, money gone, woman gone, Tiger gone!

I will have to face pain on my own now. Tiger soothed the days away. It is true I loved smoking Tiger. I didn't accomplish life on it, only existence. No writing, staying trim, the narcotic served its purpose, I didn't think of my fiancée, my money, or my future. My thoughts were plain – another smoke, sit, drink tea and think without pain while immersed in grief.

My cock is hard this morning, my first hard cock in weeks. Fantastic.

Yes, it is true I want to taste a woman again.

It is now I realize I miss Tiger because I think of my fiancée strongly now, too strongly, though it will be tomorrow that my adventure will be over and the end begins.

It is like I ate a gargantuan poison spider, lost all reason and rested on torture for reason.

Now I have theory, now I have basics. Now, I have not money, now, I have not freedom. I only have chance. Russia is my chance.

TURBULENCE

Sometimes it's stuck in the brain, this time the knife struck against my rib. The doctor said I was lucky; she must be some kind of expert, Tripfiena.

I woke in the hospital not dead as she had said, but thankfully alive with a very sore, tenderly bruised and beautifully battered chest.

The doctor said it was a skilled professionally tooled wound; he also said I'd been drugged. The drug she gave me is why

I'm here in the hospital, the dagger wounds are minor, more performance than threat. Tripfiena never intended to kill me hurt me or rob me. I still have my belongings by my bedside. It's said Tripfiena used a Russian passport at the dormitory. Maybe she is Russian after all.

The name on the passport used the name Tripfiena as a middle name.

I know where to find her. She knows I won't charge her, but to have a dagger or to take a drink in her company I'll have to think again.

True she drew blood – minimal for such an experience.

In some ways nothing feels better than servants with caring eyes. I hospitalized, I like the jesters, the importance, I like to be looked after genuinely!

Sure, it is asked if I'd like to buy a ticket and take myself home.

They can't understand, this is my home, everywhere and anywhere I am is my home. What I'd like, what I'd like is to see Tripfiena, speak with her. I thought when I woke she'd walk into the hospital and be by my side. They've said she's disappeared. I think not.

I distinctly remember her jotting down her e-mail address in my scrapbook on the morning as I drank the vodka of death. I need only read my scrapbook. I also know the city where her bank account is kept.

Immediately after I leave the hospital I look up Tripfiena's e-mail and send a message: 'Why'?

She didn't explain but two days later she sent an answering e-mail. 'I want to see you. Meet me in Thailand,' is what she wrote.

———————

I KNOW HOW QUICKLY I could take a flight and see Monik. I'm now in the South of Thailand.

Tripfiena is standing straight ahead, delightful as the executioner.

A smile I haven't seen from her, is she now just acting? I think it is herself, whoever she may be.

'So, are you Russian or Canadian?' I ask.

'I guess it's fair to come clean, I'm Russian now, and once I was Canadian. I married a Russian man five years ago. You can see I'm no longer married. I've been engaged many times. Are you mad at me?'

'No.' I answer.

'Come on, you don't have Interpol behind you, do you?'

'You may know more about that sort of thing than I do.'

'How is your money, do you have enough?' She asks.

'Enough for the month,' I smile back relaxed.

'Good, I'm glad this trip didn't break you.'

'Why didn't you take my money?'

'Maybe I should have to fulfill your dream of really being poor, near death, but I think you weren't ready for death, they would have just sent you back to Canada. I wanted to see you again. I never thought to take your money, any other man sure I would have.'

'Thank you.'

'What about Russia?'

'Russia is finished,' I answer. 'I can't afford it now.'

'I knew you'd come. I always knew you'd be a perfect man.'

'Why Thailand, do you have a boyfriend in Thailand?'

'No. I've come for a tan.'

It isn't the same. We aren't the same as before with no Mongolia, no dormitory, no two, no loneliness, here in Thailand we have many options. We settle on dinner. She's detached from the Russian accent, the coldness, the coyness, now she makes me laugh. Answers are brought forward quickly.

'I've learnt many tricks like where to put a dagger, and a drug in a drink that immobilizes a man with a huge erection. You hate me, but it is what you wanted, to die with a woman making love to you. You said you'd like to die this way. You also said you'd like to die by a drug or a weapon as you made love. So now you've done it. Did you like it? I wanted to please you. Have I pleased you? You said you've done everything a woman could do and now you really have.'

'Yes, I loved it. You are the same as Tiger.'

'What is Tiger?' she asks.

'No matter how destructive or wrong you can't stay away from it because you think it feels good. This is Tiger.'

'I'm not good for you.'

'I don't know what's good for me.'

We walk.

My thoughts are on the evening and what will become of us.

Where will I sleep, with an eye open?

What is her next trick?

I have my own room, as does she. Instinctively I can't stop myself, we hold hands and place ourselves at a bar stool. I know the beach is next and after that her skin on her bed I will climb in discomfort as a killer unable to kill, licking my prey to death.

A gin in tonic is sipped as she spells out what makes sense.

'I'd like you to go and see your fiancée. You can buy a ticket tomorrow morning. I came here so you'd be close to her. Don't be your fiancée's Tiger. Go and see her, if you don't like what you see I will be here for a couple of weeks. You can then decide if you want to stick to our plans. The plans we discussed. The plans you agreed to while I was taking all your wishes, dreams, and burying them. Now comes truth; you will stay with your fiancée or come back for me.'

'Who are you? What about your husband?' I inquire.

'I told you who I am – I'm Russian – I was once Canadian. I haven't seen my husband in over three years; we were lovers, sure. Now my husband is dead. What else do you want to know? Will I be faithful until you decide? I won't answer, I don't know. Will you be faithful? A man always wants assurance, they always want what I'm not. I always give them what they think they need.'

'Why me, what can I give? What can you take?'

'You're not happy that you met me?'

'Happy. Happy I'm alive. Happy I no longer want to die.'

'Did you ever tell your fiancée you wanted to die?'

'No. Our love was intense enough. Besides, after I met her I wanted to die with our children's children, I couldn't fathom her death or dying on her.'

'And now?'

'And now nothing – complete abandonment of theory, plans, dreams. I will start over.'

Alone.

———————

CONCLUSION

I apologize for not reaching Russia.

I didn't even reach Mongolia.

I was intercepted. I was on my way but things happen.

When you make the effort to go somewhere, a destination, dramatics will happen.

If I was to make it to Russia, I don't know where I would stand today.

Sometimes it is better to dream than to visit something, someone, somewhere.

Disappointment is missed, the dream forgot.

Hysteria seemed near life deserted me.

I wanted to desert reason. You have a story.

♟

© Les Cook

Pretty Vroom

———

SHE WAS HESITANT AND I overpowering but subtle enough to bring her relaxed into my room . . . I spoke polite, listened first.

A plastic being is nowhere near – riding what, riding who, riding my full-cock rhythm to ecstasy.

I'm her pilot to an orgasmic sky rocketing through galactic cascades.

For a moment I can't stand it. I think maybe she's an alien, perhaps a spirit.

What kind of freak is she?

My last thought before the rhythm has ceased.

I walk to the shower.

I love the shower, but I can't stand and relax in the hot water.

I just want to scream.

Disgusted, I want to slit my throat with a knife. I've been tricked and I like it. She is cunning, she is the smartest person I've ever known to do this, to trick me, but I'm smarter because I've figured it out.

She nears and I leave the shower to let her have her turn.

She can't understand my unusualness, a man who won't finish.

She looks at me asking when I will be spent. Yes, she thinks she'll finish me off before she leaves.

My big trap can't stay shut, 'You're an alien, a spirit. I've figured it out. You're not human.' I exclaim.

'What, what did you say?'

'I said, "I don't know what you are".'

'You think I'm not a person? I'm a woman,' she bawls, her voice in torture.

I take the remark back, 'Just kidding.'

She enters the shower room annoyed, and I contemplate if I'm sane.

Call it life related illness but I'm suspicious of every acquaintance and she is no different. No person can just be plain and simple. Air-flight travel, the alcohol, the scene, up all night, the extremely gorgeous woman that I can't believe has spent the night having the most wonderful sex with me has led to a strange mindscape.

Welcome to Macau – I could never expect such an experience on my third trip, but at the same time I did.

I'd landed in Hong Kong last night from North America and caught the fast ferry to Macau checked into a hotel, and then hit the town.

Out of the shower she is smiling again – gorgeous.

She lays down removes the towel so I can study her. 'You see,' displaying her pubic hair – her lips. 'You see I'm no spirit or ghost. I am a beautiful girl.'

I can feel, I can see – we make love slowly, kissing.

My hard cock glares at her outer surface, soon combing, massaging. My cock full in her – she's real. I'm not insane.

Her head is thrust up the bed against the nightstand.

Before the top of her head is bruised by the wood I lift and shift her to the end of the bed in deep thrusts that have slowed.

I eject. I have finished.

This time we shower together.

It is true I might not love her but she is compatible, unbelievable comfortable – love is one thing you know is unreal – but she is perfect so there must be something wrong, there must be something not real she's too surreal. Never can I be this lucky – can I? Is it possible?

As I reach for a towel she speaks in earnest honesty; 'You fuck me five times and still I like it. I think nobody understands you. You are . . . I don't know what you are, my first time with a man like you. Why I make love to you with no condom? I don't know why I let you, I can't say no to you. I don't know why I came here, or why I'm still here. Never before I do this, stay the night with a man I don't know. Crazy – you are crazy,' she says, finishing with a bizarre laugh as the shower room door is closed.

We are the same.

We'd started the evening with a condom. In our second session the condom wasn't placed; I sensed she was clean. I didn't care about safety – she felt good and if I died having sex with her, I'd be happy – this is how I felt. I still haven't come inside her, when will the guts come for that?

She dresses. A huge smile at the mirror accenting her words, 'I have never met a man like you, never in my life.'

I think the same about her.

My friend 74 is at the door.

74 can't believe the woman is still in my bed. 'She is still in your bed, she is beautiful. She stays here with you all night and most of the day.' This time 74 speaks directly to her and not as though she's absent from the room, 'You are very attractive.'

She visibly trembles.

'How old are you?' 74 asks her.

'Twenty-six,' is her answer.

'She's an alien,' I declare to no one but the air and the ears of both her and 74 to hear.

'No,' she shouts as she hides in the bathroom

'Where is she from?' 74 asks.

'She is Thai. Thailand.' I answer. 'But that's not what I mean by alien. I mean she is not from this world.'

'Yes, true, she may be from Thailand but she is out of this world.'

'I know.'

74 in delight; 'I see her here today and I feel like I must go fuck something – I want to have sex with a woman like her, what's her name?'

'Pretty Vroom.' I answer.

'Really?' he asks.

'Yeah really,' I answer amused.

'She is good. You slept with her?'

'Yes, she's the best.'

'I cannot believe your good fortune.'

We invite Pretty Vroom to lunch, after initially polite no's, she concedes to our encouragements.

As we walk the street she is smiling, I can't look at her for a moment, she is too incredible. In heels she is almost as tall as me with outrageous curves. I can't stand it, she is peculiar. She stands sideways off balance, irregular. From behind you'd swear she was a fashion model, but when one faces her eccentric look, you'd dismiss her as a serpent waiting waters for sex, love, money, and death. At lunch she quivers beside me clutching at my trousers that fit loose on my thigh. This I know is a sign that she loves, she can't contain her frantic clutching and the bizarre notion of what she feels inside. As Pretty Vroom speaks, one is lost, not only lost in the sounds but in the shape her mouth takes and how her lips exaggerate to an inescapable form. Her teeth are perfect so it is not a calamity, one may think she is slow if she did speak English alone as her mother tongue. 74 and I are both left stunned by her actions, though opt not to stop her in speech, but to hump her.

———————

HOW DID I MEET PRETTY Vroom? Six hours after my flight landed. I found her outside of a dance club. She was distraught tipsy, apparently hurt by a hopeful boyfriend. I walked her to her car. She'd misplaced her car keys. I hailed a taxi to take her home and paid the taxi driver to take her. I left my hotel address in her purse – she refused the taxi after finding her keys. I suggested coffee, sober up before she drove home. She conceded; we went to my room and made love like I said.

74 saw me talking with her last night but he left with another woman or alone I'm not sure; 74 was somewhat incohesive to the surroundings as well. I don't know what 74 was really up to – that is the uniqueness of 74. He was all decked out in a wool suit and tie when we met last night. Maybe he wore a hot suit, but in the cool night wind I'm sure it felt nice. We've been friends forever.

It was incredible that after months 74 e-mailed. He had an idea for us, a business together. He wouldn't tell me anything more about the business proposal on the phone or e-mail.

I replied that I would see him when I arrive in Asia. If anything, visiting 74 could be a lot of fun.

Friends started calling him 74 in his last months of high school – his favourite numbers were four and seven. Number four his ice hockey number, and number seven I don't know why. He was born in 1967.

When on a trip to Brazil with his parents, a woman who suggested she was a clairvoyant told 74 he'd lose his virginity in Brazil. The clairvoyant also said he'd have to have sexual relations 73 times if he wanted to find true love and marriage. 'Your 74th experience will be your true love, you will marry her, any lover before will not be your true love, it will be a failure.'

74 was excited about the possibility of losing his virginity. He did have a high school girlfriend who would not progress to intercourse. He'd spent almost a year in waiting and was still waiting for intercourse with his girlfriend when he left for Brazil with his parents. The clairvoyant told him 'If you have a girlfriend now, leave her – she isn't good for you.' 74 liked the sound of the clairvoyant's words; he blamed his girlfriend for holding his virginity.

74 lost his virginity in Brazil.

He returned to high school with wild stories of his trip to Brazil. He was famous; everyone wanted to go to Brazil – he broke up with his girlfriend and in her desperation, she had intercourse with him.

The name 74 stuck. He instantly loved the fame, the respect of a nickname. He cultivated this image after high school, introducing himself as 74.

By the time he was twenty-four years of age he was lingering at #22 of his sexual conquests.

He went back to Brazil.

He went back to see the clairvoyant but could not find her. He did however find a relative, a much younger attractive girl who was also apparently a clairvoyant, though not practising. 74 explained what her aunt had said. The young attractive Brazilian explained even though she is not a practising fortune-teller she could read him because she inherited the powers of her aunt. For a fee she'd read him, plus a tip if what she said became true. He paid the fee and promised the tip. She read him and concluded what her aunt had said was true. The beautiful young clairvoyant also said she would be his 24th sexual encounter.

74 thought why not #23 or better #74? He wanted her more than even his high school girlfriend.

'No,' she said, 'After me you will not have another lover in Brazil and I will be your 24th because a man cannot come to Brazil and only find one lover, so after #23 you will come back and see me.'

#23 was received later in the afternoon.

The young clairvoyant took another week to seduce – he paid the tip she'd requested. After another week he left Brazil heartbroken as he could not stay in the same country as the young clairvoyant. She'd left him heartbroken.

Before his second trip to Brazil, he didn't take the readings seriously, but after the second trip to Brazil the readings were as important as life and death.

Nobody knows if his story is true; the Brazil clairvoyant story is too good to dismiss.

74 is essentially a good guy who went wrong – his high school friends said it was after the trip to Brazil he went bad. When he returned a second time, he was lost forever in the spell of 73 dates before he could find true love.

I quite like him.

He'd near doubled the total number of sexual conquests since his second trip to Brazil.

Later in years 74 complained he was only at #47 of sexual encounters, he wanted to be in love desperately.

I spoke of my recent trip to Asia.

'You want to hear about China? After hiking Tiger Leaping Gorge, I was in need of a haircut...' I went on about a sexual encounter.

'Okay, you've sold me,' is how 74 answered after my example. He spoke up, 'I'm not going for just sex.'

'What are you going for?'

'Vacation,' he answered. 'I cannot just pay for sex because it won't count. It has to be a real experience. If she and I are both excited... yes, I can still pay a tip for the natural experience.'

'Don't worry.' I calmed him down.

He decided it was time to go Asia.

74 is now obsessed with life in Asia.

I feel responsible.

74 wandered around Asia – India to Japan. As friends we'd drifted apart. Each of us in discovery, frustrated, mystified, grateful, longing, and not wanting to tame this continent but simply be it. Now we are both desperate. He desperate to survive and I desperate to start over. I've thought to reach out to him.

We'd had an agreement – don't disrupt, sometime somewhere we'll meet and compare. He understands, at times he wants to go home too.

He told me he'd been starving in the street. He'd even let a Chinese man suck his cock for money. The Chinese man wanted to give 74 his gold watch if 74 would let him do sex in him, 74 said he didn't need a gold watch. 74 stayed with various women. One woman he stayed with was 54 years old – he was 34, she had a good place for him to sleep and eat, 74 stayed with her for one month.

I asked 74 why he didn't sell his wool suit when broke.

He answered, 'This suit is a money making and sex machine – when I put on this suit things happen. Sell this suit and I lose a chance to meet someone exciting or make love."

I agreed. I guess he's not so poor.

Salvation came when he'd made a couple of deals and some money came through from back home.

He came clean and spoke of opening a restaurant in Cambodia – he said he had the money but was afraid he'd be unable to survive the first few months and that I was the only person he could trust or wanted to trust. He could try, but I don't have any money, in debt at best.

'Can you cook?' I ask.

'Yes. If we want to stay here in this glorious life, we must do something to survive. Let's do this restaurant in Cambodia together. We will start small, sleep on the premises.'

I love Cambodia.

I ask, 'What do you want me to do besides give you all the money that I've saved?'

'I want you to go back to Canada and work. I will pay the return portion of your airplane ticket because we are partners. Work, save money, and then come back and go in the restaurant business with me. I can wait six months for you. Now I have a place to stay for free I teach a family English. I stay in their house, eat their food and two days ago I fucked their cousin, number #68, I will continue to fuck her saving myself at #68. I cannot stay like this forever as they will learn English soon enough. I told them six months, and I've been with them for four weeks already. Go back to Canada, you can make a few thousand. Five or six months from now I will have all in place, equipment, location, advertising, staff, and I will be broke.'

Nothing he says makes sense.

'And if I don't have enough money in six months?' I ask.

'Return again and again until the restaurant can survive or send money.'

'Why didn't you tell me this before I flew over?'

'Because you'd say no. You already bought your airplane ticket, took time off from your job – your heart was set. But now you have experienced Asia again and you know you love it. Take a detour on your adventure – and make it last a lifetime. Listen take another couple of weeks travelling, feel good, then accept my offer of a return ticket.'

I nod.

'In four, five, or sixth months you can start another adventure. Plus, you'll have a business.'

IT WOULD ONLY TAKE a one-day wait for Pretty Vroom to find my room, this time in the afternoon.

I only want to see her, nobody else.

I speak, 'I want to keep doing what we did the other night, have sex without protection – stay together. We can go to a clinic and get tested for disease.'

'Yes, I'd like this,' she says.

A trend started Pretty Vroom would come for afternoon visits. She'd pick me up in her sister's car and buy me lunch. Oral sex and lunch, early evening fuck then dinner, let me alone most of the day was the trend. Perfect. She seldom slept the night – she stayed at her sister's condo. Pretty Vroom liked to wake up early to be at work at her sister's cafe. She was becoming the perfect girlfriend – no complaints, sex and leave, she paid for more than half our dates. Yesterday she drove me to a massage shop and paid for a woman to massage me while she was busy at work. I guess this was the best way to keep an eye on me.

This afternoon we've toned sex to love-making.

Have I crossed the border and found what the normal have? Can I hold hard in her all day till the sun has stopped coming? I can. Is this what making love is? I want to look at her face. We exist in intercourse as with tea, television, except we focus on each other in calm delight, another position, a different movement to arouse but steady most of the time. It is funny how little one thinks in ecstasy – a thought is minimal and feelings are absolute. We are feeling beings not thinking. The only thought is to stay in trance, orgasmic. How sweet she is. After this, what more can be? Enjoy this now it will never be again. Justification, I'm man, she is a woman, we are one, she is at the same place as I am. Her eyes say what I feel. How have I become so tender? A rough man heeled to precious hands that embrace the length of her face. My eyes don't laugh as usual, they are eyes that can cry in truth – it is my first time to be peeled to a soft peach, a sweet mango. I cannot fool her in this gentleness, affectionate, this wonderment. I'd say marry me but I don't want it. I'd say love but it would ruin it. I already love it otherwise we'd be dead and done – I love what we do. When will I not pull out of her? Slowly I have begun not to pull out, sometimes she smiles sometimes she's upset.

'Do you take something to stop pregnancy?' I ask.

'No. Sometimes I'm happy that maybe I will be pregnant and other times I'm frightened I will be pregnant. I can't stop you... I don't know why.'

'Me too, sometimes I want to say I don't care and other times I say be careful.'

'Why do you think you're the star of this relationship?' she asks me.

'Because you love me,' I tell her.

'And you don't love me?'

'I love what we do.'

'Are you happy alone?'

'As long as you come visit,' I answer her.

'You can stay here, or in Thailand. You don't have to leave for Canada. I have business that you can do. I have a small apartment building, a car rental and some other business in Thailand. You could put some money in with me and we could stay like this. For the rest of your life – you don't have to do a thing but be good to me.'

'And,' I comment.

'I'm lonely.'

'Where did you learn how to make such good sex?' I ask her.

'I didn't. I've just tried things I've read. Now I practice to make you feel good. Do you feel good?'

'Yes.' I answer happily.

'You know I have been busy. I went to school, married – my husband and I separated. I work in business every day. Now I want to try everything with you.'

'No boyfriends?'

'No. I liked one man before you but he lied to me. He did not care for me.'

———

74 WANTS TO CAROUSE with me most days or have me not spend money or go to Canada fast, anything but plan my possible future with Pretty Vroom.

Slowly I'm falling in love – not the crazy no thinking love but perfect situation love, a modern economic and enjoyable love – unemotional, solid, and fantastic. What an intelligent person would consider as a good decision.

74 is leery of her plans. He doesn't want me to lose out to her. What 74 doesn't know though he may think, if things do work out with Pretty Vroom, I may go for the investment in the restaurant with him.

I think Pretty Vroom also questions 74. The other day he came to visit at the same time as her and we left him alone in my room while we went out for lunch. When we returned the chambermaid and him were engaged in a kiss side by side stroking hands on my bed. I laughed Pretty Vroom did not. 74 did pay the chambermaid attention in the past when he'd visit.

74 doesn't count the chambermaid as a number because he and her are friends and haven't ventured beyond kissing. If and when he does think he's found true love he'll visit the chambermaid to up his number to #73 quickly.

I comment, 'I don't know if the young Brazilian would accept manipulation as part of the potion.'

74 responds. 'The chambermaid is part of the potion the plan, we would be having sex already if we didn't hold back – it is not constructed our feelings towards each other. Like any lovers, if the time is right it will happen between us.'

He has many women on retainer in case he must reach #73 quickly.

I PRONOUNCE.

'My father alien. . . my mother monkey.'

Her elongated waist to neck to chin narrows to a triangle like a freaky Siamese cat, she looks up in agony, my full size in her round triangle eyes, gripping her paws to my legs, wise and soft she can't be tamed, heal as she pleases.

She cries, 'I don't want you to leave. You are good for me. I think you won't come back and you will forget me.'

'You just fucked a monkey; do you like to fuck monkey?' I joke.

'No,' she says. 'I fuck alien.' We laugh. She continues to purr, 'Sometimes I'm scared when I make love to you. I'm scared you are going to die.'

'Why?'

'Your face, the way it looks the sounds you make.'

'Like a monkey?' I respond.

'No. Like an alien,' she responds jovial.

Serious again she speaks sensitively, 'I don't want you to die.'

The television is on at 3:00 am.

She doesn't pay attention to television.

She naps – I'm alive at my peak with ape-man-like energy and intellect reflection as intense as an alien.

I go out, eat Chinese breakfast at Hotel Lisboa, fifteen-different dishes and back to Pretty Vroom as the greatest ape – smart as man, a man that feels like ape – food, sex, freedom.

Pretty Vroom wakes in reflection.

'You think like a star you want to give sunshine. But can you?'

'With you I can, though I'm no star,' I say.

I've made a decision to delay may adventure in Asia. I will fly back to Canada. If I want to continue on with Pretty Vroom I'll need money. It is best I leave now before all my money is spent.

Pretty Vroom is a chance for me, absolute love is distant, I have 74 as a friend. I can travel I can find trouble on my own and I have Pretty Vroom as a place close to call home. I can invest and make love to her until she tires or I tire and then I can move. Is she a better bet than 74? I don't know but maybe I can have both certainly both can't be wrong.

Pretty Vroom says, 'Sad is rich and happy is poor. Poor don't understand rich. The rich understand they don't want to be poor, so they are sad. Poor still have dream to keep them happy.'

'How do you know? You are not poor,' I say.

'Neither are you – I'm happy I've met you.'

'I have to get ready soon to catch my flight.'

Pretty Vroom says, 'Before you go, I want to make love standing on my head.'

After embracing, kissing, sucking, hot she stands on her head. She is the perfect length I stand on tippy toes between her legs sideways placing my cock down inside while bouncing softly up and down.

'I will come back in three months and stay in you.'

'Star,' she shouts

'Vroom, Vroom,' I appeal.

———————

PRETTY VROOM LEFT MACAU – she stays in Thailand to tend to her business.

Four months later. I fly to Thailand.

I've come back with what money I can.

Pretty Vroom can be my freedom – my peace.

74 is somewhere near too. He wants me to invest, support, and work with him. He's found a location, done the leg work, he's ready to start in a little more than a month. He could be where he was before three months from now – on the street. In some ways I envy him, throw it all on the table and go for broke. I have no need now to invest with him when I can stay quiet with her.

Pretty Vroom had a driver pick me up and deliver me to her apartment building where I'll stay.

A towel covers my waist to thighs, a tight tee-shirt on I walk to the apartment door carrying a prominent grin.

She comes to my bed.

She spits on my cock, Vroom I'm back in her hand teasing ways, coming in lovely agony.

I take to the shower singing Vroom, Vroom I'm happy to be back.

She walks around the room in a state and takes me for lunch. I haven't space or a chance to speak – after our meal she states:

'I have HIV.'

'What?'

She interrupts. 'Stop – have you been tested?'

Embarrassed I say, 'No.'

'Why haven't you been checked? You said you would.'

'I'll go today.'

'Yes, go today. I didn't tell you on the phone because you said you didn't have a girlfriend. The clinic told me to tell you. They can't understand – I needed to see you, to ask you, to tell you.'

'Ask me if I have knowingly given you HIV?'

'I don't know. I don't know what I think. But I had to see you – I needed to see you in person, hold you. I don't think you gave me HIV. It is for you I worry. I hope you have not lied – you said you don't see other women.'

'I haven't seen anyone.' I speak to her true I was busy trying to make and save money to free myself of a torturous life.

Pretty Vroom does not cry.

I can't stop thinking that maybe I have not only passed HIV to her but many others – this is the worst, a terrible moment. And if I haven't passed it to others she's passed it to me. I have been faithful to Pretty Vroom.

Die – I never thought die. I thought no more pussy ever, can't breathe it again.

This is what I thought.

At the clinic I'm close to passing out. Pretty Vroom and an assistant help me to a bed where I'm in a blur for minutes.

A doctor tells me Pretty Vroom is healthy at this time, she doesn't need medication but this could change in time. The doctor assures me to use a condom – she insists that I and Pretty Vroom must use a condom even if I test positive as well.

The Internet I go. Do research.

I have more questions than answers when I'm finished with the Internet.

Anxious – worse now – with information you can take it whichever way you like.

I'm confident of a future.

Back at the apartment I've sunk, I've sunk alone. I retreat to the bedroom.

Death doesn't ravish me – life does, what can I do?

How can I live?

Can I ever fuck again?

Can I ever suck pussy again?

Humiliation.

Let me fuck again, I beg.

I can't stay in the bedroom, thinking horrifies me.

Pretty Vroom says sometimes she doesn't believe she has it. When she tells another, she has HIV, they complicate it, answering her wish, 'No, this isn't true you are so strong so beautiful'.

Pretty Vroom lets me alone – she will pick me up in the morning for the results.

If I said I wasn't scared the night before I was to find the results – all would laugh. I don't know what my answer to life will be. I control life I believe – I look at chances, the chance that if I do test negative, I'm free to find another lover. If I test positive,

I'd still have Pretty Vroom. She would have all of my blood. I could never be with another woman.

Wicked is the mind.

Have I killed Pretty Vroom?

Calm in the morning – can't think something until you know something.

The clinic assistant greets us outside with smiles, another assistant comes out they are all smiling festive as they hug her.

Joy burst to the street.

The medical report reads L Cok. Negative.

My name spelled wrong.

I may never forget this.

Happy controlled.

I'd fucked her twenty times.

She is amazing she can't pass it on. I'm brilliant I can't receive HIV.

Genius

A person thinks as this before he has all the answers of something called HIV.

We walk out, blanker than before.

I think fuck right now.

It won't stop me it can't stop me.

I want to say now what? But she answers for me.

Pretty Vroom says, 'Go buy condoms.'

I have my answer.

She explains, 'I've been waiting months for you. If you don't want to – don't.'

It is a plain, simple, fast decision; keep having sex together with a condom. Check her health, check mine. My heart is set – not hurt her.

How many times did I check to see if the condom was still on?

Can I kiss, lick, eat?

Before I couldn't wait to get rid of the condom, now I do all I can to keep it on.

At first, I thought we wouldn't make love again.

HIV positive. I can still live with her, love her.

A part of me wishes to be equal to her, HIV positive. Just continue on as before, no condom, and if it happens, it happens.

I'm sure the day will come where I will be free sexually and then months of fear.

The reality after is much different.

I repeat – promiscuous life you've come for me, my blood.

I tell her, 'I'm not comfortable making love sometimes.'

She scolds, 'Then don't stay.'

We are looking at ourselves when we see through our eyes.

Our minds connect to each other through invisible lines.

———————

THE CRUSADE – EAT HEALTHY she already does.

I stopped drinking. She didn't drink much anyway.

Lots of sleep, she slept lots.

There is nothing I can do to help her but sleep with her.

I figure I'm safe.

The only thought is in the future can I risk sex with others while she is at work?

Sometimes I try to ask how she thinks she got HIV – she gets mad, she doesn't know.

Sometimes I think her husband passed it to her. She says she hasn't contacted him.

Other times I think she had sex when I was away and contracted it.

Another day I think it wasn't sex at all.

I'd like to talk to someone all about the disease, learn everything, and of where I should be. I haven't told anyone. I'd like to tell the world.

Sometimes she cries saying I don't love her.

What else can I do? Marry her?

I don't know why I want to stay with Pretty Vroom – it is the path I'm to take just keep doing what I had first captured? But deep inside I miss sliding sideways against her and then into her as we sleep. Now everything is slow, lotion and condom.

Once she told me, 'I think you are waiting for me to die,' if we were married, I thought.

She hasn't let me invest with her yet or has she committed to marriage and I haven't asked.

She won't allow me not to use a condom, and I won't allow myself to without a condom. She wouldn't stop me though – she'd tell me but she wouldn't stop me if I didn't use a condom. We've come close.

Sometimes I think she knew all along she had HIV– and couldn't pass it along. At other times I figure she thought it was just a matter of time before she passed it on and we'd stay as we are.

Everything changed last night when she said she couldn't see me anymore.

My month was up.

It was a surprise, troubling, even if it was also a relief.

Heartbreak is deep – anything else but this fucking secret disease.

'Go, I'm married,' she said.

'But you are separated.'

'Let me have my way. My husband has HIV. I have HIV. You do not. At times I think you too have HIV but you don't. I know you don't. Go find a woman you can make love to without worry. I wouldn't say this if I thought you truly loved me, but I don't think you truly loved me before you found I was HIV. Don't be sad I'll divorce him. I don't know why you have stayed. I love you I can't keep you in a cage, so go away.'

She is correct. I loved the idea.

74 is a phone call away. I take my money to 74 and wish him well.

Maybe we will call the restaurant Pretty Vroom.

All entertainment is in my head. As close to God as I can get . . . rip his face off, destroy his inside, I'll cater to him and in the end, I'll find his demons, death to the myth, death to tradition.

I don't want this vacation to end.

♟

© Les Cook

74

OUR STORE HAS A SMALL eatery. It really isn't much, shakes and healthy lunch, breakfast is a big deal. We introduced fortune-telling at the store. Medicinal and magical healing herbals, plus to get the ladies we discovered manicures to be a steady way of receiving clientele. Get your nails done, have your fortune told, buy some medicinal herbs enjoy a health shake or coffee, whatever your taste and if you have to wait, eat some food.

We don't have many bills except our rent, and we'd have to pay this to live anyway. Since we sleep on the premises and eat the food from the eatery, profit is used for our entertainment. If I want some privacy, we can get a decent room in a guesthouse for $15 a night. We have a nice contingent of women working at the store. 74 stays away from knocking off numbers with staff as this is his place that allows him to stay with at least a small income. Some mornings he wants marriage now, and other mornings he wants to wait. 74 is a contrasting guy with trouble written all over him, yet he treats his staff with respect. He's a partner and friend I trust, to a point.

I returned to Cambodia to watch the store while 74 took his turn and journeyed to Canada.

74 thought maybe love would flourish in Canada or at least a prospect. He said he had two sexual partners left – the second

would become his wife. He kept saying 'Two left' all happy and excited.

A day before 74 was due back in Cambodia he called from Kuala Lumpur where he was laid over. He's decided to extend his layover for a week. He's met what he calls a strong possibility in a German girl. She'd followed her boyfriend to Kuala Lumpur where he works, she doesn't work, she'd admitted she'd come to Kuala Lumpur to end the relationship with her boyfriend while at the same time enjoy herself. She spends her afternoons with 74. 74 says when she falls in love with him, he'll visit a nightclub hostess and make her #73 before having sex with the German girl – she will be his true love number #74. These are exciting times.

———

A CUTE YOUNG WOMAN came to the store yesterday discreetly asking for 74. I didn't think it was about a job. With her looks, she didn't come to our store looking for a job. This morning she's come again asking if I can have a coffee with her. I'm charmed but a little hesitant and ask how she knows 74.

'Work – I came to him before about working,' she answers.

After more discussion, it is understood she wants to discuss a personal matter about her and 74.

She is pregnant – pregnant with 74's child.

Wow, I wonder what number she is. She is sweet, very cool, a special girl. I think I'm glad she isn't #74 on his list, I'd be jealous.

We've agreed on a friendship – I'll relay the message to 74 of her pregnancy.

74 arrived in Cambodia earlier than expected with news of his own.

The German girl he thought his true love, is false. She may well have been his true love but things went astray. The German girl tricked him while they napped together. She brushed his cock as he held her tenderly. Her skirt hiked up before he could mutter a word. He wanted to wait, but she didn't wait, and he couldn't stop her.

74 was so pissed he left Kuala Lumpur the next day. He felt it was the worst fuck he'd ever had. It may not have been the worst but the expectations made it the worst.

74 is now past #73 – he can't afford another mistake. The next sexual encounter will be with his wife.

'Why so upset? You are going to find true love.' I tell him.

'Yes, but look at my last fuck, I ruined it.'

'You can find her again. How long did the clairvoyant say it would take to find your wife?'

'She didn't. It could be a lifetime or an instant.'

'Go back to Kuala Lumpur and screw the German girl for the next twenty years.'

'I should have stayed and enjoyed myself,' he answers me.

'Why do you feel so strongly about all this clairvoyant stuff?' I ask.

'Because I want to.'

'What happens if you have another sexual encounter, like say you reach #75?'

'I die.' He clearly states.

'So if you want to die at least you'll be getting laid.'

'Thanks.'

'I have something to tell you.'

I told him about the pregnant girl and then let him alone to gather his thoughts and unpack his luggage.

————————

74 CALLS THE PREGNANT girl Bella.

Bella was #72 on his list. She was a girl he said he could not resist. Bella was hired, paid for three months in advance and never worked a day. 74 said he wanted to see her more but she refused, saying she'd made the money she needed.

Everything is true – 74 had unprotected sex with Bella. He said it was part of his stipulation; Bella was #72 and damned if he was going to give it up with a condom on. She is now three months pregnant.

I'm jealous and disappointed – Bella may be too young for me, but I like her.

74 doesn't help, 'She knows you L Ce. You don't remember her. You were drinking with another girl at the time. You talked to Bella when your girlfriend wasn't in range. You wanted to meet her, you asked for her ID card to see if she was of age, the whole bit. She came to see you the next day but you were sleeping in a guesthouse. She came to see you again when you were in Canada – she didn't come around again until she asked me to hire her. Do you remember now?'

'Yes. I wanted to drop my girlfriend to be with her. Why didn't you tell me?'

'You think you're the only one interested in a pretty girl like Bella? I did tell you she'd come to see you.'

'Marry her.' I exclaim.

'I can't marry her – the next one I'll marry.'

'Are you sure you haven't lost count somewhere?'

'No, I've kept perfect track.'

'What advocates a number?' I ask.

'Any kind of sexual relationship, if the sexual organs are strongly stimulated physically by another person, it is sex.'

'If you are kissing a girl and you rub against her with your pants on, does it count?'

'Depends, every encounter is different.'

'What about Bella, you paid her?'

'Yes, I paid her in advance to work at our store. When we had sex, I could not let her work because I can't mix sex and work.'

'I think you don't have an accurate count and who decides what stimulation is and isn't?'

'I go by what the young clairvoyant told me on my second trip to Brazil. We discussed much of what a sexual encounter is. I'm not like you.'

'What do you mean?'

'You don't count fat or ugly girls but you count hot girls that maybe you only kissed.'

'So?'

'So what number are you at?' he asks.

'Four.'

'Four. You see.' He shrugs his shoulders.

'Four I care to count,' I explain, then smirk.

'You can see I'm not dead so my count is perfect.' He laughs.

'I guess.'

'If you would have been available to Bella – it would be you with the problem.'

'It wouldn't be a problem if I had a child with her,' I answer him.

WE WENT TO MEET BELLA'S sister yesterday. Bella and her sister share the same small house, they have a private garden area that makes the place relaxing. Bella's sister was taken with 74 – they had a good laugh together although 74 couldn't believe the sister isn't pretty as Bella.

'She's ugly. Her body is not bad but her face is very ugly – she doesn't have a good nose. Not like Bella. I hope our child doesn't have a face like this.' Is what 74 said.

'I dream of ugly women – not real ugly, just not the kind of women you'd think I'd dream of fucking,' I answered him.

'I'm not like you,' he said.

Bella's sister has a ten-year-old son who also lives at the house. I too was struck with the difference in looks between Bella and her older sister – it is almost cruel how beautiful Bella is. Her sister is average looking, a sexy body, but compared to Bella she has no chance.

74 is convinced he can make it all work. Bella's auntie owns the home but doesn't stay at the house much, preferring the countryside with Bella's mother and other relatives.

74 and Bella aren't having sexual relations; both are fine with this, 74 knowing true love to come and Bella just happy to have the father around with support.

74 is a regular at lunch daily at their home enjoying the cooking of Bella's sister. Cashews, chicken and greens, river fish and

coconut, vegetables, peppered prawns, curry, pumpkin soup, mango salad, the list goes on, and on. He comes back daily with stories. He's begun napping after the meal on the outdoor hammock enjoying his new family. I'm settled minding the store.

Bella has come to visit me this afternoon.

'You are a fortune-teller. I see you sometimes with foreigners giving readings,' she tells me smiling.

'I'm not a fortune-teller, I'm a consultant,' I answer her.

'How much money do you make?' she asks.

'I don't do it for money. I do it for the little bit of money they spend ordering food or drink. I do it for the store, for myself, I haven't done anything out in the world and here, I feel I do something. It does bring people in for the sake of curiosity, they buy a drink, a shirt, a snack, a medicinal treat. Spread the word. I make most of my money when I travel back to Canada and work. This place is just a way to prolong my visit to your country. A country and people I love.' I've really poured it on strong – I can't help myself, sweet as honey.

'I'd like to see what you do. Can you read me?'

'I'm not a reader. I'm a consultant.'

'Consult me.'

'No, you don't want to hear it. You don't want to listen. I won't consult you. I don't consult friends and family.'

'Why?'

'Nothing is certain just entertainment – speculation. I put on a strange suit or a striking suit or handsome clothing whatever will delight the client's mind, make what I do seem true. Do you want to come and listen? Come listen today. I have a client.'

Bella agrees we spend time together waiting for the client.

My client:

The gentleman is a travel writer on the Internet. He was referred to me. Part of his tour – seems everyone is some kind of travel documentarian.

It is agreed that Bella will sit in, I offer a discount to the client but he refuses, saying no discount is necessary for letting Bella listen. I'm sure he looks at Bella the same way as I do – a face you'd pay to stare at for hours.

The client doesn't have questions.

I ask him if I can start if he doesn't have anything to say.

He says, 'Certainly.'

I begin.

'We should raise the vulture to take care of our own death remains – we raise animals to eat, how about raise animals to clean our death? Eat insects, nuts and seeds, greens. Sometimes I think I'm not green, but if I look at the way I live with little electricity... yes, I watch television. Without television, I can't argue or learn. A person thinks they're is smart if they don't watch television; smart green they think.'

I stop speaking. Let him have a chance. He must have some comments.

Nothing is said.

I begin to speak again.

'So I have my food. Now what about police? We police ourselves, no more turning a blind eye – sure there will be the secret group breaking the rules and splinter groups but essentially it will be business and not crime – the petty will be gone, undignified too.'

'Who makes the rules?' the client asks.

'Parents, neighbours, aunts, uncles, teachers. When a person is raised the rules are absorbed as natural – you can raise adults too, corporations do it all the time. But still how to decide on what is a rule? I'm a consultant. How you decide rules I don't care – I've given you choices on how to live – you will have to pay me again if you want answers on how to apply these traits. So do you want to pay?'

'I may want to pay you for amusement but your ideas are crazy.'

'It isn't much, buys me lunch today. Think of it as buying me a cold beer.'

'Sure, why not, this will be cheaper than buying a beer because I don't think I'd stop at one.'

I continue, 'If you want to impose rules on people – you only have to make them happy.'

'Fair enough. And how can you make the skeptical happy?' he asks.

'Singing and dancing – it is that simple – party. All these regimes try to stop dancing, singing, parties, or they have alcohol at the centre of happiness, but you don't even need alcohol, just some sort of tasty drink and good tasting food. The kids have to be involved too – the kids dance, the old dance, the young dance, sing, act, play. That is all. Whenever there is free time, dance – make it accessible – not strict dance schools – take the professional out of the equation. Sports, don't deny anyone of play. Let the builders build, the inventors invent the scientist's science. Play games. Competition, but not professional, not money motivated, but for fun.'

'No Olympics?'

'When the next community or friends or distant relatives come, it is the Olympics. A gift of gold for arriving, do you understand? Not business motivated – these power guys today have fools for entertainment and now the fools have turned the spectators into fools for paying to watch them. All manipulated, you can do the opposite too. Stop work and kick a ball, exercise, exercise the mind, and you will have a happy workforce doing an unhappy job. Let men and women flirt – sure you will have romance and heartbreak. You have unhappy if you hide the fun too.'

'Good. So this is what you say to people?'

'Yes sometimes, it depends, to whom I'm talking. Today I'm consulting you, so I talk this way. Nothing is certain except fun. I have two dreams at night, one is ice hockey and the other is women. I have two nightmares, work and money. Take the nightmares away. Have fun at work and supply money. How do you supply money? I don't know, but someone does know. I say different things to different people. I said these things to you because it was the easiest today as you didn't expect much though you may write lots. Sometimes I tease, ask for a tip to reveal more, it is part of the game – entertainment, a reflection of life.'

'Thank you, it was worth it. How does a tip sound?'

'That depends on you.'

'A tip it is.'

'Sounds good, bring a friend, listen for free. You will have more of an idea of what someone hears – because you came here to believe nothing. Usually, a person will ask questions or explain a problem, visit the future or past. But you didn't speak.'

When the gentleman leaves Bella says, 'I want to go dancing with you.'

'Yes, when?' I answer.

'I don't know. Wait, I will tell you when I'm ready.'

Hesitant she continues, 'What you spoke to this man. Is this how you consult people?'

'No, only him,' I answer.

Now it is my turn to ask a personal question.

'Why did you go stay with 74 before, why did you sleep with him?'

'A family emergency, my family needed money fast and he was friendly to me. I thought he could help – and not far from our house. I came to see you but you were not there. It would have been with you, my first choice. He said you were gone . . . not coming back. Will you take me home now?'

We drive to her house.

At her house my eyes are surprised, I can't believe the sight – Bella's sister is washing 74's hair, he's smiling, laughing, they're joking back and forth, she has a tremendous laugh. I find her attractive because of the way she acts.

Bella takes me around the backside of the house to her room to show me photos. It is happening and I can't stop it. It takes all my energy not to touch, not to kiss her. I have to move away.

'Help me,' she says.

I undo her top back buttons. She undresses to put on her comfortable around the house clothing. Only her bra and underwear on, her belly let out – all the while the sweetest face smiling, blushing. She dresses in front of me. She is supposed to be shy – she isn't.

We go back out to the garden where 74 and her sister are. The sister is now giving 74 a head and temple massage.

'Are you coming back to the store?' I ask 74.

Bella's sister answers for him.

'No, he has to stay here until we eat, and then tonight, maybe I let him go,' she laughs. 'He is always hungry – maybe he eat me, ha, ha, ha.'

———————

BELLA'S SISTER SURPRISES me. She's come to the store to speak with me while 74 is at her house napping.

'I've put a spell on 74, he cannot see.' Blunt, she speaks.

'What, what did you say?' I ask not sure of what I've heard.

'The food I cook, he is falling in love with me.' The sister speaks.

'What about Bella?' I ask

'My sister loves me more than him.'

'The child,' I ask.

'My sister is young and beautiful. She can have more children, a richer man or a man who she loves in the heart. It is difficult for me to find a good man. I have child already and I'm getting old. Tonight, you will take my sister out and I will be out with 74.'

'What does 74 say?'

'You will not talk to him. You will come to see us tonight. 74 will wait at our house, he can wash there – he has clothing at our house he can wear.'

True, she's been doing his laundry. She does everything for him. She's been seducing him.

'You come tonight if you want my sister happy, 74 happy, and you may be happy too.'

'What about the baby?'

'I will look after the baby when it is born. 74 will do anything for you, Mister L Ce.'

'What do you want me to do?'

'See my sister.'

My erection is strong in thoughts of Bella.

In the evening we go out – 74 and Bella's sister dance, drink, laugh. Bella and I sit and watch – we don't speak, we have one slow dance. Our foreheads touch as we kiss on the dance floor. We walk off the dance floor holding hands. Bella's sister has spied us, she rushes us out of the club holding mine and 74's hand. She doesn't stop holding 74's hand on the drive home. Bella cuddles with me.

At the house we sit outside in the garden. Bella and I stay outside while 74 and Bella's sister go inside the house to make drinks.

After some time, Bella encourages me to check on the drinks. I enter the house. 74 is standing behind Bella's sister next to the counter where the drinks are supposed to be made. He's rubbing her beneath her dress while his lips are on her neck – her eyes closed, her chin up and neck extended, she is in bliss.

They both briefly notice me at the door. She places his hand on her breast. I turn and walk away. I close the door. There is nobody in the house, they are alone, her son was sent to the countryside earlier in the day to visit family.

Planned perfectly.

'No drink?' Bella asks.

'Somebody is busy.'

Bella's smile is stifling. Her hands are on me as I join her on the bench. We are slow.

'We have all night,' she whispers.

We have begun to make love on the garden bench. She is in control. If I die tonight, fine.

It is happening, sure it is happening, I'm making love to a pregnant Bella. The spell is bound. I have become a part of it. 74 is making love to Bella's sister in the kitchen of the house, I can hear them as we pass around the back of the house to Bella's room.

In the morning as I sit alone in the garden, 74 joins me.

He says, 'I can go back and have sex with any of the 73 other women I've had before – but none of them would be as good as a wife as this one will be.'

'Good point. I guess the clairvoyant never said anything about cheating?'

'She never said.'

'Do you still have the number or address of the young Brazilin clairvoyant?'

'I'd never let you have her – she was the best.'

Bella's sister cooks us lunch, as good as the food looks, I won't eat.

'Don't be scared.' Bella says. 'This food will be good for you.'

I eat the soup, thinking what kind of spell will become of me. I know I can't stop Bella easily.

'Do you cook?' I ask Bella.

'Yes. My sister teaches me.'

Great, I think sarcastically.

Time to find a wife.

I go back to Canada before the baby is born.

I go to make money so I can return.

A healthy baby girl is passed on to Bella's sister and 74 to raise as if it was always theirs.

74 said Bella was a replica of the young clairvoyant in Brazil.

Very cute.

Thank you

Just a book of tales.

Go back to sleep.

Did you love *Tempting Fiction*? Then you should read *The Program Illusion*[1] by Les Cook!

[2]

Do you like escape? From self-imposed retreat to world venture.

Travel with a freethinking man, and a woman free to think.
Year 2000. Isolation Spa – Art of Confusion.
Damascus – Peshawar – Kashgar.
Bratislava – Vancouver – Phnom Penh.
And the lot in-between.

---

1. https://books2read.com/u/mddVyy

2. https://books2read.com/u/mddVyy

About the Author

I relish my privacy in real life as I give much experience in the stories I tell. **Les Cook**